"You want me to leave!"

Kate was shocked. Did Nick hate her that much?
Unconsciously she pressed her hand to her throat.
Of course he hated her. She had been Jeremy's wife,
and he had hated and resented Jeremy.

"Go back to where you belong, Kate. This is a harsh
world. It's not for a young woman on her own. A
woman like you needs more out of life—close
friends, company, comforts...perhaps, in time,
even a new man...."

She recoiled...not so much at the thought of a new
man, but with guilt, because only moments ago she
had found herself reacting to another man...the
last man on earth she ought to be reacting to!

Elizabeth Duke says that her main interest and love is writing, although she's awfully fond of traveling, too. She's visited almost every state in her native Australia, and has traveled to New Zealand, the U.S., Canada and Mexico, which leaves her with no shortage of fascinating settings for her romance novels. The author is married and has two children.

Books by Elizabeth Duke

HARLEQUIN ROMANCE
2833—SOFTLY FLITS A SHADOW
3034—ISLAND DECEPTION
3110—FAIR TRIAL
3200—WILD TEMPTATION

OUTBACK LEGACY
Elizabeth Duke

Harlequin Books

TORONTO • NEW YORK • LONDON
AMSTERDAM • PARIS • SYDNEY • HAMBURG
STOCKHOLM • ATHENS • TOKYO • MILAN
MADRID • WARSAW • BUDAPEST • AUCKLAND

ISBN 0-373-17161-7

OUTBACK LEGACY

CHAPTER ONE

'LET me *go*!' Green eyes blazing, Kate writhed and kicked, struggling to free herself from the overseer's suffocating embrace.

'Come on, gorgeous...' The man's sun-wrinkled face was unbearably close, the coarse stubble of his chin grazing her cheek. 'You know you want this as much as I do. You're a red-blooded woman...you must get real lonely now that you're a widow lady...'

Rage, repulsion threatened to choke Kate. 'If you don't let me go, Leif Clancy, you're out of a job!' she threatened, but he was deaf to reason, his pale eyes glazing over with lust.

'Don't you worry, sweetheart, there's no one to see us...' Backing her against the rough trunk of a coolibah tree, he brought one hand up and pushed aside her wide-brimmed hat, fumbling at her hair until it came loose from its confining ribbon and spilled in a glossy golden wave over his fingers. A hungry light leapt to his pale eyes, and, as she tried to avert her face, he seized her hair and tilted her head back, bringing tears of pain to her eyes. His hot breath was on her face, heavy with the smell of stale tobacco, and as she gasped for air he muttered thickly, 'I've dreamed about this...about having you in my arms like this... Don't fight me, babe!'

'Let me *go*, damn you!' Kate spat the words out, repugnance curling her lips as his moist, sensual mouth raked across her cheek, seeking her lips. Summoning what little authority she had left, she commanded imperiously, 'Think of Annie... your wife!'

He paused momentarily, his pale eyes wavering. 'Annie needn't know... this'll be our little secret.' A wheedling note crept into his voice. 'Let me show you what you've been missing out on, Kate. I know it's what you want, deep down. You wouldn't have ridden out here alone with me if you hadn't wanted me, felt something for me——'

With a snort of loathing, Kate ground out, 'I rode out here with you to check on the bore well—nothing else! I was making sure you were doing your job properly.' Keep talking, she thought desperately. Some of it might just get through to him. 'I want to get more involved with the day-to-day running of the place, now that Ramsay Downs is my sole responsibility. What I've seen so far hasn't impressed me. Things have become... slack.'

'Whose fault is that?' growled Leif, bristling. 'No one wants to speak ill of the dead, but if the place is run down, you can blame it on your——'

'It's not my husband's fault!' Kate denied swiftly, loyally. 'It's *yours*. Jeremy left you in charge...too much, it seems.'

The overseer's lip curled back from his stained yellow teeth in the grimace of a smile. 'If you say so, ma'am,' he leered, his hard-boned body pressing her back until she felt the rough bark grazing her spine. 'I admire a woman with a bit of spirit. But face the facts, sweetheart... running a cattle station is no life for a woman all alone. You need a man, Kate—a *real* man.'

'I don't need *you*, Leif Clancy! And if you don't let me go——' The rest was lost in a muffled gasp as his fingers grasped her hair more tightly, jerking her head back and crushing his mouth down on hers, his other arm pinning her to the tree.

Powerless for a moment, she felt alarm snake through her. They were half an hour's ride from the homestead, with no other stockmen anywhere within call. What a fool she had been to ride out here with him...and worse, to let him grab her before she could even reach for her stockwhip. But she had never dreamed that Leif would try anything like this, would risk his job as overseer, would put his marriage to Annie at risk. Annie mightn't be the most alluring wife in the world, but she earned good money as Kate's housekeeper and Leif had always seemed fond enough of her.

Gathering her strength, she began to squirm and twist in his grasp, managing finally to wrench her mouth from his, tears of pain springing to her eyes as the movement almost tugged the hair from her head. She felt him release his grip at last, but her relief was short-lived, her breath catching in her throat as she felt his callused fingers fumbling with the front of her shirt, tearing at the buttons, groping at the soft swell of silky flesh underneath.

'Leif, cut that out, damn you!'

He merely chuckled and clamped her to him again, silencing her protests with his lips, even more forcibly this time, his bristly face almost suffocating her. Just as she was beginning to seriously panic, she was astonished to feel his hands suddenly loosen their grip, watched in disbelief as his head whipped back and his lean body spun away from her. She heard his startled gasp, 'What the——?' a split second before a fist crashed against his jaw, sending him reeling into the dust.

Kate staggered back against the trunk of the coolibah tree, her hands automatically flying up to drag the front of her shirt together, her breath coming in ragged gasps. She felt a dim flare of satisfaction at the sight of the overseer sprawled on his back in the red dust, shaking his head as he tried to rise, his eyes blurred, a hand coming up to rub his jaw.

Then he was blotted from her view as a dark shape loomed over her and a strong hand gripped her arm, steadying her. Slowly she lifted her head, her dazed eyes focusing on her rescuer. He towered over her, tall, broad-chested, deeply bronzed. A man she had never seen before in her life.

She reached up unconsciously to drag her hat back on, pushing her tumbled hair back from her face. Where on earth had the man sprung from? She caught a slight movement and let her gaze swivel round, her eyes widening in mixed reaction at the sight of a big grey horse drinking from the freshly cleaned trough. It looked suspiciously like Silver, one of her own horses!

'Are you all right, Mrs Ramsay?'

His voice was low, velvet-edged. As her gaze swung back to face him, she was suddenly acutely aware of the warm, steady hand still clasping her arm. So he knew who she was. But who was *he*?

She found she had to tilt her head back to meet him eye to eye. She felt a tiny jolt as her bemused gaze was swallowed by a pair of the darkest, most compelling eyes she had ever seen, shadowed by thick black brows. With an effort she dragged her eyes away from his, taking in the arrogant slash of his nose, the deeply tanned skin, the firm jaw. A face that wouldn't be easy to forget.

'I—I'm fine,' she stammered, uneasily aware of a strange tremor pulsing through her. Sheer reaction ... Leif's onslaught must have shaken her more than she would care to admit. 'Th-thank you for—for——'

'For saving you from a fate worse than death?' His tone was gently mocking, but when he saw her wince, as the word 'death' reminded her suddenly of her recent loss, he was quick to add, 'Sorry... bad joke,' as if he understood. Yet how could he?

He still hadn't removed his hand, but strangely, instead of feeling repulsed, as she had with Leif Clancy, she found herself trembling faintly under his touch.

'You're *not* all right.' Swift concern showed in his face. 'I can feel you trembling. You'd better sit down.' He lowered her gently into the tussocky grass. 'Wait here!' he commanded, and swung away from her, striding back to confront Leif just as he was rising groggily to his feet. The dark stranger stood over him, his face grim as he rasped, 'I want you packed and ready to leave by the time we get back. You'll have your wages paid up to date, and that's all you'll get. No references. Nothing. You're history here—understand?'

Leif faced him belligerently, though his eyes were wary. 'Who do you think you——?'

'Get going!' The stranger's voice was like the crack of a whip—and equally effective. 'Now...while you still have the chance! And thank your lucky stars I'm letting you off this lightly. It's a damn sight more than you deserve!'

Leif hastily backed away, tossing a sullen look over his shoulder at Kate as he hauled himself on to his horse. Hearing no counter-order from her, he angrily spurred his mount into a gallop. As he disappeared in a cloud of dust, Kate rounded on the stranger.

'How *dare* you?' she burst out, scrambling to her feet and planting herself in front of him, her eyes flashing green sparks. 'This is my property and I'll run my own affairs, if you don't mind! It's up to me to hire and fire my staff. And to decide if I give a reference or not. Not you—whoever you are!'

He inclined his head in mock contrition, and answered with a quirk of one eyebrow. 'Who am I? Looks like I'm your new overseer.'

Her jaw dropped. 'You...you're assuming an awful lot. I don't even know you. Or...or where you've worked previously. I don't take anyone on without a reference!'

To her consternation, he laughed. A sardonic, un-ruffled laugh. 'You'll find that my credentials are im-peccable. You could ask the Stantons if you're in any doubt.'

Kate eyed him dubiously. 'You know Ted Stanton?' The Stantons, Ted and Bernice, were her nearest neigh-bours, owners of Doon-gara, an extensive sheep station to the south.

He nodded. 'I know the Stantons very well—though I haven't seen them for some time. I haven't been in these parts for...quite a while.'

Her eyes narrowed at the sudden chill in his voice. But his expression was inscrutable, the dark eyes shadowed by the thick brows and the broad rim of his Akubra hat.

'You—you came here looking for a job?' Why was she stammering? And why did she have the unnerving sensation that he was the one in control here, the one with the upper hand? This was her land! All hundred thousand acres of it!

'My reason for coming here can wait until we're back at the homestead,' came the frustrating reply. 'If we don't start back soon, it'll be dark before we get there. Let's go, shall we?'

Her mouth opened again, and snapped shut. He was being insufferably autocratic and domineering, but what he said made sense, and she'd be a fool to stand around arguing. It *was* getting late, and they had quite a ride back to the homestead. And besides, she ought to be grateful to him for coming to her rescue. She *was* grateful. But she was puzzled too, and faintly uneasy, though she wasn't sure why. He was so unlike the usual stockman or outback drifter who bowled in from time to time looking for a job. Though he was dressed in the classic stockman's garb of tapered moleskin trousers, Western shirt, elastic-sided boots and broad-brimmed hat, and though he had the air of a man who knew the outback well, there was on the other hand a sophistication about him, a polish that suggested he was as much at home in the city as he was in the outback. At a guess, a well travelled man, well educated, and quite possibly successful. So why in the world would he want a position as an outback overseer, working under someone else? And a woman, to boot! There was something here that didn't add up...

For the first time Kate became aware of how isolated and vulnerable she was, out here alone in this remote part of the station with this dark, mysterious stranger who had popped out from nowhere. What did she know about him? Nothing! Other than that he seemed to know the Stantons. And he could have heard their name from anybody. If she stood around arguing with him, she could well end up having the same trouble with him that she had had with Leif Clancy.

Best to hold back her questions, and any protests, until they were safely back at the homestead.

'Who gave you permission to borrow my grey?' was one question that did pop out as she mounted Dixie, her spirited palomino.

He shrugged, unfazed. 'One of your stockmen. The one who told me where I'd find you. Can't recall his name.'

Won't, you mean, Kate thought with a twist of her lips. He wouldn't want whoever it was getting into trouble.

The hot central Queensland sun was already sinking fast in the cloudless blue sky and gradually losing its earlier punch as they headed back to the homestead across the vast timber-studded plain. They barely exchanged half a dozen words on the ride back, Kate prodding her mare into a canter whenever he came too close, to avoid having to make conversation. She saw him looking intently around, and sensed his silent criticism at the state of the fences and the poor quality of some of the cattle, and when one of the gates creaked on its hinges as they passed through, but he said nothing, and neither did she. He's blaming me, she thought, pursing her lips. And it was true that the final responsibility rested with her. She was the one in charge. But there simply hadn't been enough time yet, or enough men to spare, to deal with all the things that needed attention.

As the white homestead gates—in need of a fresh coat of paint, she realised with her new heightened awareness—finally came into view, she dropped back to let him come alongside, asking coolly, in an attempt to regain the upper hand, 'I suppose you have a name?'

His answer was brief, unenlightening. 'Most people call me Nick.' He leaned back in the saddle, running his eyes speculatively over her delicate oval face and slender figure, and she felt herself flushing under his arrogant scrutiny. 'What possessed you anyway,' he demanded into the sudden silence which had fallen between them, 'going out there alone with that creep? You were asking for trouble!'

'How was I to know he was going to—to——?' She broke off irritably, tilting her chin. 'Look. This property belongs to me. I can go anywhere I like—with whomever I choose. I—I could have dealt with him, if you'd only given me the chance,' she added recklessly. 'I don't carry a stockwhip for nothing!' Sheer bravado, she thought ruefully, reaching up to jerk at the brim of her hat, wanting to shade her eyes from his gaze.

The heavy eyebrows shot up. 'You may own this property, but you obviously don't know much about life in the outback—and what the heat and the isolation can do to some men. If you did you wouldn't put yourself into a situation where something like that could happen. Not with a man like that, at any rate.'

Stung by the reprimand, she snapped back, 'Leif Clancy happens to be married to my housekeeper, Annie—he's not exactly starved for a woman's company! How was I to know he was going to suddenly leap on me?'

She flicked her tongue over her lips, and swallowed hard as his expression abruptly changed, his brow lowering, his mouth tightening, the dark eyes glinting with an emotion she would have sworn was anger. Why *anger*?

'Your housekeeper?' he repeated harshly. But before he could say any more, and before she could question him, their attention was caught by a flying figure, as a young woman in a loose floral dress came running across the yard from the direction of the overseer's house. As she came to a halt in front of them, they saw that her thin pointed face was streaked with tears.

'Leif says we have to go...but he won't tell me why,' she burst out, gulping back her tears. 'What did he do? Tell me!'

Kate bit her lip, inwardly cursing Leif Clancy. The girl looked distraught, as if she knew in her heart what had happened and wanted to hear that it wasn't true. Leif doesn't deserve Annie, she thought with a sigh. She might not be the world's greatest beauty, or have a particularly colourful personality—in fact, this was the first time Kate had seen her show any emotion at all—but she was a loyal, devoted wife to Leif, and a good worker, who pulled her weight in the marriage.

'He——' She hesitated, casting around for inspiration. She didn't want to have to tell Annie the truth. Leif obviously hadn't told her—which seemed to indicate that he still had some regard for his wife's feelings. It was just possible he might have learned his lesson, that her angry rebuff and the stranger's intervention might have shaken him into changing his ways. If she could manufacture some careless indiscretion...something relating to his work...

'I'm afraid it's my fault,' she heard the dark stranger drawl from behind her right shoulder. It was all she could do not to whip her head round in stunned surprise, clamping her teeth down on her lip in wonder at what might be coming. 'I'm related to the family, you see, Annie—it is Annie, isn't it?—and I've come here to take over as overseer. To help Kate...Mrs Ramsay...to run the place. Which sadly means that Leif has to go...I'm sorry, my dear, but we simply can't keep him on.'

Related? Stunned as she was at this further revelation—or was it as fabricated as the rest?—Kate was swift to take up the lead he had given her.

'Leif will find another overseer's job, Annie,' she soothed. 'I'll give him a reference... naturally.' She said this with a faint touch of defiance, for the stranger's benefit. Repulsed as she had been by Leif Clancy's advances, livid as she had been at the breaking of the trust she had so foolishly put in him, she didn't want to destroy his chance of finding work elsewhere... if only for Annie's sake. He wasn't such a bad worker, and he'd always got on well enough with the men.

'And you needn't leave until morning,' she added for good measure, determined to show the stranger who was in command here. 'Nick——' somehow she managed to roll the stranger's name off her tongue as if she had used it all her life '—can stay at the Big House tonight, Annie... He can have that spare room in the jackaroos' wing.' Deliberately putting Nick into the same category as the two young jackaroos who were currently staying at the homestead. 'Nick can move into the overseer's house tomorrow, after you've gone,' she added, to make sure that her new overseer—*if* she decided to keep him on—knew that tonight's hospitality was only a temporary arrangement. And perhaps she was crazy to offer him even that. What did she know about him? Nothing! Except that she had a funny feeling, a curiously ominous feeling, that he meant trouble, even though so far he had done nothing but get her out of awkward scrapes. He was a man with secrets, she suspected... a man with a past...and, worse, he told lies with a facility that added to her unease. Related, indeed! He *must* have made that up. She had never seen him before in her life! He'd just said it to fob Annie off.

'Oh, thank you, Mrs Ramsay... Thank you!'

The sight of Annie's relief was worth the little subterfuge, Kate mused. She just hoped Leif would appreciate it—and mend his ways in the future.

'Your dinner is in the oven, all ready to heat up,' Annie said, smiling brightly, eager to please. 'I'll go and speak to Leif. I'm sure he'll feel better when he hears that you're willing to give him a reference, Mrs Ramsay...he seemed to have the idea you weren't going to give him one. That's why I thought he'd done something awful... But now I realise he's just upset at having to leave.'

'I'll have your wages ready to collect in the morning...yours and Leif's,' Kate advised Annie. 'And references for both of you. I'll miss you, Annie,' she added, summoning a smile of her own. And as Annie, still beaming, skipped away, Kate inclined her head for the stranger to follow her, her eyes telling him ruefully, And now, thanks to you, I'll have to find another housekeeper. Would one of her stockmen, she wondered with a sigh, have a wife who would be suitable—and agreeable to take on the job?

'Where are your things?' she asked, wondering if he'd brought luggage, or if he was simply carrying a swag. Not that he looked the swaggie type. Strong, tough, accustomed to the outback, but—no, hardly the type who would travel around with only a swag on his back. 'And how did you get here?' she demanded. 'Where's your car?' He didn't look the type who'd be driving a battered old ute either. Some flashy vehicle, most likely— or the latest model four-wheel-drive.

'I flew in. I left my things in the Cessna,' came the smooth reply.

She blinked. He had flown himself here by plane? His own, presumably. Even Jeremy hadn't possessed his own plane—though they'd always kept the airstrip well maintained for visitors, and for the flying doctor, and for those times when they had chartered a plane for their own use. Who the heck *was* this man? And why did he want to be her new overseer? It didn't add up!

'I'll send someone to fetch them,' she offered faintly, turning away.

'No need. I'll get them myself—after you've shown me which room I can have... for the night.' There was a whimsical note in his voice that brought her head round sharply. She would have sworn by his tone that he was amused at some private joke. But his face was impassive, the dark eyed hooded.

'Follow me,' she commanded, her own face set in equally impassive lines.

The homestead, known as the Big House, was a rambling bush timber and iron building, with wide verandas along three sides. Like the gates and fences, it had seen better days. Jeremy had promised to make improvements, and at one time had eagerly planned to turn one whole section into a nursery wing, only all that had changed when... Kate shook off the memory, and with a faint sigh led the stranger to one of the spare rooms in the north wing—well away from her own quarters—and invited him to join her for a drink on the veranda in half an hour, giving him time to settle in and freshen up first. And at the same time giving herself a few moments alone to come to grips with the sudden changes that had been thrust upon her, and were already threatening to turn her life upside down. As if she didn't have enough to contend with already!

She was conscious of a tingly feeling at her nape, a faint stir of expectation, almost of excitement, as she relived that moment by the bore well when the stranger had swept to her rescue... feeling again, despite herself, the touch of his firm warm hand on her arm, and wondering at the tremors that had shaken her as they had stood face to face. She hadn't been this aware of a man since she had first set eyes on Jeremy.

She felt in better control of herself when she emerged half an hour later, freshly showered and wearing a clean shirt and cool ankle-length trousers, to find him already waiting on the veranda, his compellingly male frame slumped in an armchair, his long legs stretched out in front of him. He had changed too, and the effect was startling, his red shirt enhancing the dark glow of his eyes and deepening the tan of his face, the open neck revealing the even deeper tan of his throat, and his head, hatless now, showing a crop of black rumpled hair.

'Don't get up,' she said quickly as he started to rise. She felt less threatened with him sitting in a chair than towering over her. 'Beer?'

'Sounds good.'

She held back her questions until they were both comfortably settled and sipping ice-cold beers from chilled pewter mugs.

'Now,' she said, crossing one slim leg over the other, and gripping the handle of her mug a fraction tighter, 'Tell me what brought you here.'

She would have sworn she saw his chest heave in a hidden sigh before he spoke.

'I came to offer you my condolences,' he said steadily. 'I'm your brother-in-law, Dominic Ramsay. More often known as Nick, these days. Jeremy's brother—well, to be strictly correct, his half-brother.'

Kate recoiled as if he had struck her, spilling froth from her mug, and not even noticing. 'You're Jeremy's brother?' She stared at him in disbelief. 'But you're not——'

'Not black...no.' The dark eyes were derisive.

'That's not what I——' Her cheeks flamed. She had been about to say, 'You're nothing like I imagined you.' Jeremy had described his brother as dark, ugly, swarthy. He was dark, certainly—deeply tanned, hair black as night, with eyes to match—but swarthy? Ugly? Most women would see him as wildly good-looking. Not handsome in the classical sense, but with those compelling black eyes, those strong features, that powerful physique, and a presence that emanated command, he was arrestingly male, arrestingly attractive, to say the least.

His voice swept in, his tone mocking, deliberately brutal, his intention obviously to make her squirm. 'Oh, I'm sure if you look very closely, you'll see the signs you're looking for. Which is only to be expected, since my natural father was part Aboriginal. As I'm sure you're well aware. Jeremy was always eager for people to know that, although we both shared the same white mother and were brought up as brothers, *he* was the sole legitimate son of Logan Ramsay.'

Kate moistened her lips before she spoke. 'You still hate him, don't you?' she breathed, staring at him with burning, reproachful eyes. 'Jeremy said you'd always hated him—all his life. Hated and resented him.' She felt a rush of pain and anger. 'You didn't even bother to come to his funeral! Not that I was surprised,' she was quick to add. 'It just proved to me how little you cared for him.'

'I didn't come to his funeral because word didn't reach me in time.' Nick's voice was low, even, as if deliberately holding himself in check. 'I was in China, as you must know, doing some consultancy work for the Government in a remote part of the country. By the time I heard, it was too late. I came back as soon as I could.'

'Not out of any love or respect for your brother!' Kate flashed back, bitterness throbbing through her voice. 'Surely,' she demanded scathingly, 'you weren't expecting him to leave you anything in his will?'

'Hardly.'

Something—his lack of reaction, the way his eyes were mocking her, his arrogance, *something*—sent a wave of fury through her. She sprang to her feet, and stood accusingly over him. 'How dare you have the nerve to come back here after... after what you did to Jeremy?'

'Oh, yes?' His eyes didn't even waver. 'And precisely what did I do?'

He was going to make her spell it out. The arrogant, insensitive——

'You tried to turn Jeremy's father against him, for starters. You deliberately burned down a valuable barn and planned it so that *he'd* be blamed for it! But it backfired, unluckily for you. There was a witness. And so *you* were the one your father—your *stepfather*—sent away in disgrace, not Jeremy. You cut your own throat!'

'My... your husband certainly did a thorough job of brainwashing you, didn't he?' In a slow, easy movement, Nick raised his beer mug to his lips, tossed back his head, and drained the contents. 'Hanged, drawn and quartered without a trial.'

His infuriating calm only incensed Kate further. 'You're *denying* it?' she gasped. Stupid question! Of course he would deny it—he'd deny anything she threw at him. Now that Jeremy and his stepfather were no longer around to refute whatever he said. 'I won't hear a word against my husband,' she warned him, breathing hard. 'That would be typical of what I know about you—to denigrate Jeremy, and try to twist things around to make yourself look good, now that there's no one to speak up against you.'

He looked up at her from his chair, his dark eyes actually softening, losing some of their intensity. 'Kate, I haven't come here to denigrate your husband. I admit we were never close, but I have no intention of saying anything against him—least of all to you.' He reached for her hand, and, much as she wanted to snatch it back, she found for some incalculable reason that she couldn't. It was as if an electric current had fused their hands together, momentarily paralysing her.

'Kate, I'm sorry if my coming here has upset you. I came here to offer you my sympathy and support... and to do what I can to help you.' There was a throb of sincerity in his voice that fooled her for a second into believing him. His fingers were still clasping hers, and there was something about them, the feel of them, so warm and strong and yet in some way so gentle and protective too, that made her want him to keep them there. Then his grip tightened on hers, and she had the alarming, exquisitely exciting feeling that he was going to pull her down into his lap. And for a brief, crazy second she found herself actually wishing that he would, so that she could bury her face in his shoulder and seek solace there. She had had to be so strong, so self-contained, so much in control, ever since she had decided to stay on at Ramsay Downs and try to achieve Jeremy's dream—*their* dream—on her own.

'If you want to be angry, Kate, go ahead—let it all out. I understand how you must feel.' Nick's voice, low and vibrant, pierced her consciousness. 'You've lost the person closest to you... your husband... after far too short a time together, and I know that must be hard. Don't think I don't know how you feel, Kate. I've lost people too...my mother, my father, my stepfather, and now my brother too.'

She blinked at him. 'Angry' was the only word that penetrated for a moment. Anger, a second ago, she realised in shocked dismay, had been the last thing on her mind! Ashamed at the way she had weakened, appalled that it should be Jeremy's despised brother, of all people, who had brought on the weakness, she reacted sharply, snatching back her hand at last and seizing on the last phrase he'd uttered. 'Oh, don't pretend that you're sorry about Jeremy,' she cried scathingly, her eyes darkening with pain. 'There was never any love lost between you—never in all your lives! You hated him. You—you even tried to kill him once!'

'Oh?' Nick's voice was ominously quiet now. 'You have proof of that, have you?'

'You know there was nothing that could ever be proved,' she whispered. 'But Logan Ramsay—Jeremy's father—knew it was no accident. That's why he kept the two of you apart...why he sent you both to different boarding-schools and sent you away to university later, and off to other cattle stations in your vacations. And it's why he watched you like a hawk each time you did come home. Because he was worried about his son's safety! And he had cause to be worried, because on your last visit home you took your revenge on Jeremy by trying to frame him for something he didn't do, hoping Logan would send *him* away. Only it didn't work, did it? You were caught out. And this time you were sent away for good!'

Nick had no answer to that. Which was as damning as any admission.

'Tell me the real reason you've come back,' Kate breathed, scraping her hands together in an effort to rid herself of his touch. Her eyes flared suddenly, then narrowed. 'Of course!' She slapped her thigh. 'It's Ramsay Downs, isn't it? Your old home. You want it back! You think now that Jeremy's gone, his grieving widow will want to sell up and get out!'

That was it. It had to be! He wanted Ramsay Downs, and he would do anything, tell her anything, to get it, even twist the truth if need be to make her doubt the stories she had heard about him. Well, Dominic Ramsay, she fumed silently, you can think again! I'm nowhere near as helpless and gullible as you think!

She stood over him, quivering with anger. 'If that's what you want, you can forget it. I'm not selling!'

For the first time she saw a faint flicker in the coal-dark eyes. She felt a flare of triumph. Something had got through to him at last.

But when he finally spoke, it was about another subject entirely.

'Where's Minya?' he rapped out.

CHAPTER TWO

'MINYA?' She stared at him blankly for a moment. 'Oh...yes.' Logan Ramsay's long-time housekeeper, Minya...the Aboriginal woman who had helped Logan bring up the two boys after their mother had died so tragically. 'Minya...isn't here any more,' she said awkwardly, knowing from what Jeremy had told her how close Nick had once been to Minya. Understandably, being so young at the time he had lost his mother. And being...who he was.

'What do you mean, isn't here?' A muscle twitched at the edge of Nick's jaw. 'She's not——'

'No, no, she's fine,' Kate said quickly. 'She's at Doongara now. With the Stantons.'

'At Doon-gara? What the hell are you talking about? She's been here at Ramsay Downs forever...she'd never leave!' His eyes hardened. 'Not voluntarily.'

Kate's eyes swerved away from his. 'There was a...a disagreement.'

'Between Minya and Jeremy.' It was a flat statement of fact rather than a question. When she made no comment, he rasped, 'How long ago did she leave?'

'I...about eighteen months ago.'

'How long have *you* been here?'

She swallowed. 'About...eighteen months.'

'Hmm.'

It was plain he thought she was to blame. The new bride, making her presence felt, making a clean sweep of the place, turfing out the ageing staff...

24

'It's not what you——' she began, and clamped her lips shut. How could she tell him the truth? Minya had been like a mother to him—far closer to him than she had ever been to Jeremy. And it was obvious Nick still had strong affection for her. '*Ouch*!' She flinched as Nick caught her arm, his strong fingers—no gentleness there now—digging into her flesh. 'What in the——?'

'Tell me!' He thrust his face closer, his eyes glowing like hot coals. 'And I want the truth. All of it!'

'All right!' She shook off his hand. 'It was...' She hesitated, darting her tongue over her lips. 'It was because of something she did, the first day Jeremy brought me here. She...stole something Jeremy had given me.'

Nick's face darkened. '*Stole* something? That's bull! Stole *what*, for heaven's sake?'

Kate's slender fingers tensed in her lap. 'Just a—a bracelet. Jeremy found it in her room. I—I didn't want...' She let the rest trail off, not wanting to appear disloyal to her husband. She started again. 'Jeremy said it would be best if she went. The work was getting too much for her anyway, and she—she didn't have the same affection for him—for us—as she'd had for you. Being——' She faltered.

'Being of the same blood,' Nick assisted baldly.

'Being dimly related,' she amended with a quick lift of her chin. 'Jeremy said she was your father's aunt or——'

'Cousin,' Nick corrected curtly. He sat forward, frowning. 'Do you realise what you've done—you and my precious brother? Hell, Minya's lived here nearly all her life! She was a young girl when she first came to work here. My father, Kim—my *real* father,' he explained harshly, 'came to Ramsay Downs after Jeremy was born, as Logan's overseer. Logan spent a lot of his

time away from home in those days, and his wife Sophie
and my father Kim had an——' He broke off, scowling.
'But I'm sure you've heard Jeremy's version of all this.
So...Minya's at Doon-gara now. Doing what?' he rasped.

Kate thrust out her chin. 'Light duties—nothing too
taxing. The Stantons already had a housekeeper, but they
were prepared to...overlook what she'd done, and take
her on.' She added defensively, 'I'm sure she's been
happier there with them than here at Ramsay Downs
with people she doesn't——' She paused, compressing
her lips.

'With people who didn't like *her*,' Nick cut in roughly.
'Hell, I didn't think even Jeremy would stoop to this—
to kicking Minya out. She was practically a mother to
us when we were both growing up!'

Kate was quick to leap to her husband's defence.
'Jeremy said she always favoured *you*...which would
be only natural, of course, after what happened to her—
to your——'

'To my father?' Nick assisted coldly. 'Minya never
blamed Logan Ramsay for my father's death. It was an
accident—a tragic, flukish accident. Logan started the
fight, sure, when he found out about Kim's affair with
his wife, but he was as horrified as everyone else when
my father stumbled, hit his head as he fell, and was killed
outright. There was an inquest, naturally, but there were
witnesses who spoke up for Logan and no charges were
laid. Logan did everything he could afterwards to make
amends. He adored Sophie, even when he found out she
was expecting Kim's child, and when I was born he
brought me up as his own son. He blamed himself for
Sophie's lapse—he was much older than she was, and
he wasn't always in the best of health—he suffered from
diabetes. He'd known from the time Jeremy was born

that he was incapable of giving Sophie another child. He was incapable even of being a proper husband to her...'

Kate had turned away to stare across the yard at the windmill, red-tinted against the brilliant evening sky. As Nick paused, she turned back and said with an involuntary rush of compassion, 'Logan must have been heart-broken when his wife died, leaving him with two young boys to bring up. How old were you at the time? Five, wasn't it?'

A brief nod. 'And Jeremy was nine.'

Kate shivered. 'Jeremy told me what happened. That your mother drowned after jumping into a dam to rescue you after you fell in. As Minya grabbed you and pulled you out, Sophie slipped back under and disappeared, and nobody could find her until it was too late.'

'And for the rest of his life Jeremy held me personally responsible for her death,' came the drily muttered response.

'That's not true!' Kate denied, turning on him. 'If it hadn't been for Jeremy, *you* would have been the one who drowned. It was Jeremy who called out for help when you fell in. And yet you never once showed that you were grateful to him. Jeremy never blamed you for her death ... he was *hurt*, if anything. You were always jealous of him, he said, because he was Logan Ramsay's son and you weren't.'

'I'm sure Jeremy must have said a lot of things about me.' Nick reached calmly for the beer bottle at his side and refilled his pewter mug.

His coolness, his indifference stung. 'Oh, don't flatter yourself!' snapped Kate. 'He rarely mentioned you!' Not quite true, but she wanted to wipe that insufferable smugness from Nick Ramsay's face.

'He didn't? Surprise, surprise.' Mockery was heavy in his voice.

'You do still hate him, don't you?' Kate accused, a faint tremor in her voice. 'You hate him because Logan Ramsay—and your mother too, before she died—always favoured Jeremy!' She turned away, her eyes misting. And it was no wonder...Jeremy was the first-born, the golden-haired, lovable one, Logan Ramsay's own son...while Nick—or Dominic, as Jeremy had always called him—had been the dark, brooding, difficult one, whose jealousy and spite had made him an outcast in the end, banished by his own family.

'And don't tell me you had any feeling for Logan Ramsay either,' she added, flicking Nick a scathing look. 'You didn't even go to *his* funeral—the only father you ever knew! But you made very sure you were back in time for the reading of the will!' Her lip curled. 'You didn't deserve Logan Ramsay's generosity. Receiving all those shares...all that money...on top of the first-class education *he* paid for. You don't know how lucky you've been. I suppose poor Logan felt guilty because he'd killed your father and felt he owed you something.'

'Yes, I dare say you're right,' Nick agreed, still infuriatingly calm, refusing to bite. 'For the record, I happened to be in South America when Logan died, investigating a new irrigation system. It was Logan's solicitor who contacted me—*after* Jeremy had rushed the funeral through without bothering to wait for me to come back. OK, OK.' He held up his hand as she tensed, ready to flash back with a disclaimer. 'I promised I wouldn't say anything against your husband. Truce?' He looked up at her, the depthless black eyes holding hers for a long, compelling moment, and to her dismayed astonishment she found herself nodding, felt her anger melting.

'We'd better go in and eat,' she said, turning abruptly away. She had learned to despise Dominic Ramsay for what he had done to Jeremy over the years, and her body's treacherous reaction to him appalled and confused her. 'Danny and James, our two young jackaroos, have just come in,' she said, relief brightening her voice as he heard their voices in the hall. 'They always eat with us. With me,' she corrected, avoiding Nick's eye.

Nick unfolded his long frame and stood up. When he spoke again, his voice had lost its hard edge. 'Look, I know what you think of me... what Jeremy must have said about me. And I can't pretend that we were ever close. But, Kate, we've got to put all that behind us. I'm here to do what I can to make things easier for you. It's the least I can do.'

She paused at the doorway. 'Why would you want to do that?' she asked suspiciously. If he wanted Ramsay Downs for himself, wouldn't he rather see her struggle and eventually fail, so that she would be more likely to want to sell up?

He advanced a step closer, and she found herself leaning against the door-frame, as if in need of its support. 'We're family, Kate, whether you like it or not. And Ramsay Downs still means a lot to me. I don't like to see the place going downhill... and, from what I've seen, it is. Oh, I'm not blaming you,' he added hastily as her eyes snapped to his. 'You can't work miracles. It obviously didn't get into this state overnight, and it's going to take time. But you do need the help of someone with specialised knowledge and experience.'

'Are you implying that Jeremy neglected the place?' she asked tautly, unconsciously straightening, and taking a step away from him.

He lifted his shoulders. 'I'd say it's been going down-hill for some time...before Jeremy even took it over. They tell me my father—Logan—was much sicker to-wards the end than he ever let on, and maybe he let things slide. I'm not blaming Jeremy. He was away a lot of the time, from what I've heard, following the polo circuit.'

Kate couldn't deny it. That was how she had met Jeremy in the first place. At an equestrian ball. She had been one of Australia's top show-jumpers at the time they met, as mad on horses as Jeremy. But she had given up her show-jumping career—as well as the business career her stockbroker father wanted for her with his own lucrative family company—to follow Jeremy on the international polo circuit, marrying him in Hong Kong after a whirlwind courtship, and spending the next few months flitting around the world between India, England, Argentina, Barbados, and a host of other countries, watching polo matches by day and socialising every night. They'd had a ball. She had been just nineteen, and starry-eyed about her dashing new husband, and Jeremy had spoiled her, treating her like a princess. In those days, they hadn't had a worry in the world.

'Jeremy gave up the international polo circuit when his father died,' she informed Nick crisply, pulling herself up to her full height as he moved a step closer to *her*. She was disconcertingly aware that the top of her head barely reached his shoulder. 'Jeremy and his father were very close... Logan must have missed his son terribly when he was away from home so much,' she heard herself gabbling on. 'But Logan always knew that Jeremy would give up the polo circuit in a flash if anything happened to him. Ramsay Downs always came first with Jeremy.'

She glanced up at Nick's face, thinking he was about to say something, but he merely nodded and waited for her to go on.

'I'm sorry I never met Logan,' she admitted, her eyes growing pensive. 'We were planning to stay with him for a spell on our return to Australia, but when my parents met us at Sydney Airport they gave us the terrible news—that Logan had died of a heart attack—caused by his diabetes, apparently. Jeremy flew up to Ramsay Downs immediately to organise the funeral and take over the running of the station. I joined him a few days later.' Jeremy had urged her to stay with her parents in Sydney until he had matters sorted out and the house fit and ready for her inspection.

'You'd been to visit Ramsay Downs previously, though, hadn't you—before you married Jeremy?' Nick asked curiously.

'No, I hadn't,' she confessed. 'I'd never even been to the outback before, except for a trip to Alice Springs once with my school. But I fell in love with the place straight away,' she added, a defensive note in her voice.

'No doubt you saw it through the rose-tinted spectacles of the brand-new bride you were,' Nick remarked, not unkindly.

She flushed. 'No, it was more than that. I felt...' She bit her lip and added shyly, 'I felt straight away as if, in some way, I belonged here, as if I'd come home. I've never really been mad about city life, or the business world my father was trying to draw me into, or the stuffy social lifestyle my parents and friends always seemed to find so fascinating. I always preferred to spend my holidays, when I could, at my uncle's stud farm, rather than in Sydney... I've been crazy about horses all my life. I wouldn't give my parents any peace until they bought me a horse, and let me learn riding and dressage, and later show-jumping. I worked for my father after I left school, in his stockbroking firm, but it was really only to save up enough money for my show-jumping, and the travelling. Ramsay Downs... the outback... well, right from the very first minute I saw it, I loved it. I loved everything about it.'

'The isolation never bothered you?' Nick asked curiously. 'The heat, the dust, the flies?'

Kate gave a faint smile, and shook her head. 'They're all a part of it. You come to accept them. I love the outback, I always will. Something takes over in your body...you become a part of it.' The isolation had never induced loneliness in Kate, but rather a feeling of freedom and peace. Jeremy had taught her to adapt her expert horsemanship to the demands of mustering wild cattle, until she had equalled his skills, and in an amazingly short time, for a city girl—a 'townie', as Jeremy had sometimes jokingly called her—she had had the frontier in her blood, and the restless bush had become a safe and comfortable home.

'Jeremy was so happy to be back,' she recalled aloud. 'He didn't miss his polo at all.' She flushed faintly, her lashes sweeping down over her eyes, not wanting to admit that he had taken it up again later—or why. 'He was so keen to get back into the swing of things and start building the place up again.' That had been Jeremy's dream... to see Ramsay Downs back to its former glory. Only he hadn't lived to see his dream come true. Even before his tragic accident, their lives had started to fall apart...

Tears pricked at her eyes, and when she spoke again her voice had sharpened. 'I'd better go and serve up the dinner. The two lads will be clamouring for their tucker.' She swung away from him at last. 'I'm sure you know where the dining-room is.'

'I'll come and help you serve it up,' Nick offered, surprising her—and at the same time bringing a quick frown to her brow. She didn't want Nick Ramsay's help, in the kitchen or out in the yards—or indeed anywhere on Ramsay Downs. His presence was a constant reminder of the pain and suffering he had inflicted on her husband over the years. But how was she going to refuse it? She mightn't want it, but she couldn't deny that she needed it. At least until she found a permanent replacement for Leif Clancy and was able to convince her brother-in-law that she could run the place without his help.

'Danny Styles and James Macquarie, our two jackaroos... Danny, James, I'd like you to meet my brother-in-law, Nick Ramsay.' Kate kept her tone light as she made the introductions. 'Nick will be acting as overseer until I find a replacement for Leif Clancy. Leif's moving on in the morning.'

The two young men looked surprised, but knew better than to question her. Danny, a good-looking, athletic young man just out of agricultural college, was the brighter and better educated of the two and would no doubt succeed in whatever field he ultimately embarked on, while the easy-going James, heavier, chubby-faced and cheerful, was solid and dependable and a willing worker who would be a boon to any station that took him on.

'What about Annie?' James was asking.

'Annie will be leaving too...naturally.' Kate avoided Nick's eye as she passed the pepper and salt to James. 'I'll have to rustle up another housekeeper from somewhere.'

'I'd like to fly over and pay my respects to the Stantons in the morning,' Nick put in smoothly. 'If Minya agrees to come back,' he added, dropping his voice so that only Kate could hear, 'would you have any objection?'

She hesitated before answering. She had always felt bad about sending Minya away, but, on the other hand, Minya had been close to Nick in the past, and to have the two of them here at Ramsay Downs, the two people who had the least affection for Jeremy, to see them pairing up against her—Jeremy's widow—even plotting together perhaps to drive her away...she'd be crazy to——

'I'll fly over there with you,' she heard herself answering, her tone brisk. 'If Minya's to come back, the invitation should come from me.' And if Minya showed the faintest sign of antagonism, or if she seemed perfectly happy and settled where she was, she could always change her mind before issuing the invitation.

'Fair enough.' Nick obviously sensed he'd made a victory and didn't want to jeopardise it by arguing with her.

There were the Stantons to consider too, of course, Kate mused. They might not want to let Minya go. She would have to sound them out first. It had become second nature to her to tread warily with the Stantons. Polite as they had always been to her face, she had never felt quite comfortable with them. But perhaps that would improve now that Jeremy was no longer...

Swiftly stifling such thoughts, she said pleasantly, 'Bread roll, Danny?'

For the remainder of the meal they chatted about station matters, with Nick asking a lot of questions of the two young jackaroos—too many, Kate decided with a flash of resentment. As overseer, he had a right to ask, she had to concede, but there was something about the way he was going about it—as if he was already taking over, already calling the shots, secretly making decisions that ought to be hers. After all, she was the boss here.

'We can't afford to do that just now,' she intervened at one point, only to have Nick quietly point out, 'You can if you cut down on the number of stockmen you have here.'

'But I can't do that——' she objected, only to have him wave her into silence.

'You can if we make use of the Cessna. By using my plane to help with the mustering and to flush out any stragglers hiding in the bush, I could do the job of three men, and in half the time. It would also be an economical way of inspecting the station.'

She protested. 'Jeremy always said you can't beat a good stockman for mustering. I'm well aware that some people might think we're behind the times not using planes or helicopters, but I agree with Jeremy. Planes and choppers scare the cattle to death.'

'They soon get used to it...so long as you're careful not to drive them too quickly so they end up exhausted or you separate the calves from their mothers. And as long as you make sure that you give them a bit of time to settle down after they're brought in.' Nick reached for a bread roll and began to butter it. 'A small plane won't worry them nearly as much as a noisy chopper.' He pressed on persuasively, 'You'll still need horsemen on the ground—not only to bring the cattle into the yards, but out in the paddocks ready to get to work when I've told them where to find the stragglers.'

'And how do you propose to do that, from up in a plane?' she asked scathingly.

His lip quirked. 'Any number of ways. I can radio, or drop notes to them, or buzz the area. Then after the muster, I'll fly over every centimetre of the paddock in search of any beasts which have still evaded the muster. Stockmen can waste hours—days—doing that on horseback. The plane can also be used to check the fencing. There's little point in doing a clean muster if other cattle can stray into the paddock through a broken fence.'

He seemed to have all the answers! Kate managed to sit out the remainder of the meal in polite patience, but when the two jackaroos left them, one offering to clear away and wash up the dishes, the other to make coffee and bring it out to them on the veranda, she faced Nick defiantly.

'I would like to make it perfectly clear, Mr Ramsay, that no matter how many changes or improvements I agree to implement as a result of... any suggestions you make, I don't really think that you—that I——'

'That we'll ever make a happy, unified team?' he taunted softly, leaning back in his chair and thrusting his thumbs into his leather belt. 'No, perhaps not. Jeremy and I always had the same problem, which is why my father—as Logan Ramsay brought me up to call him,' he was quick to add, catching her swift look, 'decided against making us partners after his death. It would never have worked. But things have changed now. Jeremy is no longer here. And you...' He paused, letting his dark eyes slide over her in such a way that she felt herself flushing. With anger, she thought defensively, not with embarrassment—and certainly not with pleasure. 'Why would an attractive young woman like you want to stay on out here in the outback without a man, without children...? You *don't* have any children, do you? A son, perhaps, that you'd eventually like to see grow up and take over here?'

She found she was gripping the edge of her chair, her knuckles showing white as she fought down a wave of painful emotion.

'No, I don't have any children,' she managed to reply. Jeremy would have loved a son. Right from the start of their marriage, while they were still following the polo circuit, he had talked about the day when he would hold their son in his arms. But no son had come...and no daughter either. That had been the greatest regret of her brief two-year marriage. She felt she had failed Jeremy in the one thing he had wanted above everything else.

'Well, you didn't have much time,' said Nick, and the sympathy in his voice was even harder to take than his derision.

'Time enough,' she said bleakly, rising from her chair and leading the way out on to the veranda. Time enough to see Jeremy despair of her ever falling pregnant. Time enough to see a doctor, to have tests, to find out that there was nothing physically wrong to stop her from conceiving. Her doctor had suggested that Jeremy come in for some tests too, but her husband had reacted sharply to that suggestion, as if she were putting his manhood into question, declaring that there was nothing wrong with him and he didn't need to have tests. And she hadn't insisted, hoping that more time was all that they needed, and blaming herself when Jeremy threw himself back into the local polo scene and rarely came near her, rarely touched her after that. She had still hoped that things would improve in time, but there had been less time than she had dreamed...

James brought out their coffee as they were settling into armchairs on the veranda. 'Mind if Danny and I go and watch the video Smithy brought out from town?' the lad asked, and when Kate smilingly shook her head he bade them goodnight and withdrew, leaving the two of them alone.

'Tell me,' Nick said a few minutes later as he took her empty cup from her and set it down on the side table, 'how did it happen...Jeremy's accident?' He reached out to rest his hand on hers as he asked the question. 'I heard that he was killed playing polo. That came as a shock—he was a crack horseman, one of the best. So how did it happen?'

Kate found herself staring at the hand covering hers, at the strong, well-shaped fingers, the brush of fine black hairs on the tanned skin, and found herself dimly wondering why its touch made her feel so good, when she ought to be repulsed by any contact between them. This was the man who had always hated Jeremy, who had tried to hurt him, blacken him in his father's eyes, destroy him. This was the man who had waited until both his stepfather and his half-brother were dead before coming back to the home he had left under a cloud, before coming back to claim Ramsay Downs for himself, as if he believed he had some right to it now that they were gone.

If he had been closer to his brother in Jeremy's lifetime, it might have made a difference, she might have sympathised and been tempted to come to some arrangement, perhaps even considered going into partnership with him—or even handing the place over in its entirety. But knowing what Nick had done to Jeremy, knowing how Jeremy would turn in his grave if he had any idea that his brother was here trying to gain possession of Ramsay Downs, made her stiffen her resolve. He could stay here for a while ... he could even help her get the place back on its feet—it would only be making up in some small way for what he had done in the past—but after that ...

She shook her thoughts away and answered his question. Bleakly. 'He fell off his horse and ... broke his neck.'

Nick's fingers tightened on hers, and she winced in pain and snatched back her hand at last as he muttered disbelievingly, 'Broke his *neck*? *How*, for heaven's sake? Jeremy's taken tumbles before—plenty of them. Even the best rider can take a toss occasionally, especially playing polo. But Jeremy knew how to fall without causing serious injury. So how could he have *broken his neck*?'

Kate's tongue flicked over her lips. 'Apparently he ... blacked out before he fell.'

'Blacked out? In hell's name, *why*?'

'They said he went into a diabetic coma.'

'Jeremy was a *diabetic*?'

She nodded, pain deepening the green of her eyes. 'It came as a shock to everyone. I don't know that even Jeremy himself knew. He hated going to doctors...hated the thought of being sick. If he did have any suspicion about it, he must have shut it out of his mind, not wanting to face up to it. He—he certainly never said anything to me.'

'And you never noticed anything was amiss?'

She caught Nick's frown and thought, He can't believe I didn't know, or suspect. *His own wife*. She looked down, studying the hands in her lap. So much made sense now... in hindsight. Jeremy's concern about his manhood... the way he had pushed himself so hard, living every day as though it were his last... the many times he had come in tired and thirsty after a long hot day out mustering or working with his polo ponies, too worn out to make love to her. Only at the time she had blamed herself, thinking he'd lost interest in her, that he had turned away from her because she hadn't been able to give him the child he had so badly wanted.

'No,' she said with a sigh, unconsciously twisting her hands, one over the other. 'I never for one moment thought...' She shook her head, admitting in a muffled voice, 'Maybe he lived too well, pushed himself too hard. But he never appeared to be ill—even though the doctor said it must have been coming on for some time...'

She stared pensively at her hands, her eyes glazed, unseeing. Despite the way Jeremy had worked and played himself into the ground in those last months, he had always impressed her with his energy and fitness, had always looked the picture of health. He had been a superb horseman, a fearless, daredevil polo player. It was hard to believe there could have been anything wrong with him. She had been so young and inexperienced when they met—barely nineteen—and he had been in his thirties and at the height of his polo career—such a dashing figure on the polo field, so handsome, so tanned and golden-haired and charming, that she, flattered by his attention, impressionable, and as horse-mad as he was, had fallen head over heels in love with him.

She tried to conjure up his face in her mind, as he had looked in those early months of their marriage, before the bitterest disappointment of his life had brought harsh lines to his mouth and an evasive sadness to his eyes.

Even before that, way back, there had been something, a hint of vulnerability, a deeply buried melancholy under the sophisticated exterior, that she had found curiously endearing. She had always suspected that it had been put there by his half-brother Dominic, who had hurt him and borne a grudge against him all their lives. But in hindsight, aware now of the diabetes that he must have secretly suspected, secretly dreaded, knowing his father had been a victim of the same disease, she wondered if it had been more his buried fear of the disease, of becoming less of a man than he felt himself to be, that had injected that faint underlying melancholy. A melancholy that had later, when he had failed to become a father, turned to bitterness and despair.

Nick's voice cut through her thoughts. 'But he did give up the international polo circuit after Logan died.' There was a faintly puzzled note in his voice.

She raised eyes drenched with unshed tears. 'Oh, yes, he did. He said now that Ramsay Downs was his sole responsibility he wanted to settle down here permanently and—and raise a family. He had all kinds of plans for the station . . . renovating the homestead, making repairs, improving the stock, buying more polo ponies and breeding them in a big way. For a while he didn't even play polo locally—he wanted to spend every day here, building the place up.'

'Then what happened?' Nick asked bluntly. 'By the state of things here, he obviously didn't carry out too many of his plans. And yet he did take up polo again, obviously.'

The implied criticism in his voice raised Kate's hackles. 'A man needs some relaxation. We'd had a severe drought to contend with, and a flood to follow, and— and other problems.' Not wanting him to seize on those 'other problems', she challenged swiftly, 'Surely you're not denying a man the right to some relaxation?'

'Certainly not,' he said, and yet a dubious, questioning note still hovered in the air.

She sighed, and asked, tight-lipped, 'Would you like to have a look around? And meet some of the men?' She glanced at her watch. 'After that I have some bookwork to do. We don't keep late hours here... our days normally start at dawn.' She shot him a look that said loud and clear that she hoped he would be up to it, that his comfortable city lifestyle and his overseas travelling hadn't softened him up too much.

'I'm used to early starts,' was all he said, as he rose to follow her down the steps from the screened veranda into the rose-scented garden and across a narrow stretch of spongy green lawn—a lush oasis in the midst of the vast golden plains and scrubby bush that surrounded them.

Kate paused to wonder if she was being a gullible fool allowing Nick Ramsay to stay on here, even temporarily. Then she shook off her doubts and told herself sharply that she could deal with Nick Ramsay. After all, forewarned, surely, was forearmed.

CHAPTER THREE

FOR some time now they had been flying over the open downs country of Doon-gara sheep station, with barely a tree to break the seemingly endless blanket of Mitchell grass below. On one solitary tree they spotted a flock of sulphur-crested cockatoos, adorning the branches in splashes of white and yellow; sheltering under another, a herd of kangaroos. Kate took a deep breath as the Cessna banked sharply and swooped towards the station airstrip, sending sheep scattering below.

'Sorry if I scared you.' Nick had noted her sigh. He wasn't a man who missed much, she was fast discovering.

'I'm not scared,' she answered unthinkingly.

'Then why the big sigh?' He gave a quick frown. 'You're not having second thoughts about asking Minya to come back, are you?'

'No, of course not.'

'Then what is it?' He shot a narrowed look at her. 'The Stantons?'

She shifted edgily in her seat. The man was too perceptive for his own good! 'Why would you think that?' she hedged, unable to deny it outright. She always felt this same faint discomfort, each time she visited the Stantons.

'I thought, since Jeremy was once married to their daughter, you might feel a bit awkward with them,' Nick spelt out.

So he knew! 'That was a long time ago,' she said, bracing herself as the Cessna roared towards the runway,

43

its wheels touching the ground with a slight jolt. As they bumped over the uneven ground, she added defensively, 'Abigail has since married again, so why should there be any awkwardness? She and Jeremy weren't married for very long,' she reminded him. 'Barely a year. They should never have married in the first place, Jeremy said. They simply weren't suited.'

'No... perhaps not.' As he brought the plane to a halt and cut the engine, Nick glanced out of the window. 'Well, looks as if we have a welcoming committee.'

A dusty white Range Rover was bouncing over the rough ground to meet them. As it pulled up in a cloud of red dust, Kate saw that both Ted and Bernice Stanton had come out to meet the plane. Ted, white-haired and built like a tank, towered over his petite, stylish wife as they stepped out of the vehicle and hurried to meet their visitors as they climbed down from the plane.

They greeted Nick as if he were an old friend, which surprised Kate. Time, of course, could dim old memories, and it appeared that the Stantons had decided to let bygones be bygones. Or maybe they simply didn't care what Nick Ramsay had done to Jeremy in the past—Jeremy never having being a particular favourite of theirs, since his brief, ill-starred marriage to their daughter.

Which Kate had always considered rather unfair of them, Abigail being every bit as responsible as Jeremy for the break-up of their marriage. The two had simply drifted apart, by all accounts, realising very quickly that they had made a terrible mistake. But the Stantons, being Abigail's parents, would understandably be biased.

Ted and Bernice drove them back to their gracious colonial-style homestead, and after making them both comfortable in their elegantly furnished open-style lounge-room, plied Nick with questions over hot buttered scones and tea, brought in, not by Minya, but by the Stantons' regular housekeeper, Ivy. Of Minya there was no sign, which didn't surprise Kate. The Aboriginal woman generally kept out of sight on the rare occasions Kate came visiting—and had been even more conspicuously absent on the even rarer occasions in the past when Jeremy had accompanied her.

Pushing the thought of Minya to the background for the moment, Kate found herself listening entranced to Nick's tales of his work in South America and China and other countries he had visited, and his extensive travels in the Top End of Australia, initially gaining knowledge and experience, and in more recent times sharing his expertise and giving advice to others, as well as buying and selling land and stock.

It came as a surprise to learn that Nick already owned vast tracts of land up north, and more than one cattle station, as well as business interests in Sydney. So why, she wondered, would he be so interested in getting his hands on Ramsay Downs as well? Sheer greed? The need to expand his empire? Sentiment? Ha! She scoffed at the notion. Even though he'd made that comment about Ramsay Downs still meaning a lot to him, Nick Ramsay simply didn't strike her as being the sentimental type. From what she knew of his past, he was too malevolent, too calculating, too grasping for sentiment. And besides, he had caused nothing but trouble whenever he had been at Ramsay Downs, and had been despised for it, so how could his memories be warm or pleasant? Unless it was those very memories—*bitter* memories, mingled with a warped sense of revenge—that lay behind his apparent desire to secure the property for himself. A determination to possess what he had never been able

to possess during Logan's or Jeremy's lifetime. The need
to finally win, to have the last laugh!

Now that, she thought virulently, did make sense.

'And how is Abigail?' Nick was asking pleasantly.

Kate, burying her speculation, noticed the way Bernice
glanced at her husband before she answered. 'Oh, she's
fine. But, sadly, her marriage...' She broke off with a
sigh, and Ted swiftly took over.

'Abby will always have a home here... at Doon-gara,'
Ted said gruffly. 'Anyway, Doon-gara needs her. Bernice
and I aren't getting any younger, and with Teddy Junior
working up north, gaining valuable experience, we need
Abby here to help us run the place. Even when Teddy
comes back, the property's big enough for both of them.
They can run the place in partnership. And then Bernice
and I, knowing it's in good hands, can happily retire.
We're thinking of building a smaller place for ourselves
on the coast—a nice little retirement cottage.'

'Abigail's...coming home?' Kate asked carefully. She
had never actually met Jeremy's first wife. Abigail hadn't
come to Jeremy's funeral with Ted and Bernice, sending
flowers instead and a short note of condolence. After
her divorce from Jeremy, Abigail had found a public
relations job in Sydney and settled down there, eventually
marrying a rich city tycoon. 'Let's see how long that one
will last!' Jeremy had scoffed at the time. 'Abby's simply
not cut out for marriage!'

It seemed he had been right.

'She says she might be home by the weekend,' Bernice
said, brightening. 'It'll be so lovely to see her again! I'm
sure you and she will get on well, Kate, despite...' She
coloured, her hands fluttering upward in confusion.

'I'm sure we will,' Kate assured her, and gently
switched the subject, wanting to get down to the business

which had brought her here in the first place. 'Bernice, Nick and I were wondering,' she began, as if she and Nick were of one mind on the matter, 'if Minya would like to come back to Ramsay Downs...' She paused, carefully picking her words. 'Annie, my housekeeper, and Leif, my overseer, left us this morning, and Nick— well, both of us... we'd be pleased if she came back. If you're agreeable, that is. And Minya too, of course.'

Well, I've done it, she thought. No turning back now. I hope Nick is satisfied.

Bernice was smiling, not just at Nick, but at her too— the warmest smile Bernice had ever given her. 'I think Minya would be delighted,' she said warmly. 'And no, of course we have no objection. Minya belongs at——' She broke off awkwardly, as if she had remembered why Minya had come to Doon-gara in the first place. But there was no underlying censure in her voice as she added, 'Why don't you go and ask her yourself, Kate? She's in the kitchen. Nick, you go too. She'll be so happy to see you back.'

Nick waved Kate on. 'I think you should speak to her first,' he suggested. 'I'll come in a few minutes.'

Kate nodded, hiding her surprise—she wouldn't have labelled Nick a diplomat—and excused herself, swallowing hard as she pushed open the kitchen door and came face to face with a startled Minya.

She hadn't changed a bit. Still the same slight build, the same look of wiry strength, the same white bobbed hair, the same brown weathered face. Her eyes, dark slits in her crinkled face, were wary.

'Hello, Minya.' Kate summoned a smile. Even if the woman did agree to come back, what if she still held a grudge? What if she was openly hostile? Once she knew that Nick was back, wouldn't she side with Nick, against *her*? And perhaps even aid and abet him in trying to drive her out?

'Hello,' the Aboriginal woman said curtly. She had a voice like cracked nuts, deep and rasping.

Kate swallowed. 'I suppose you've heard that Nick has come back for a visit?' Best to let Minya know straight away that Nick might be leaving again. *Would* be leaving again, she corrected herself resolutely. At Minya's cautious nod, she added, 'He's anxious to come and say hello to you. But first I wanted to ask you, Minya, if you would consider coming back to us? Annie has left us, and I'm going to need some more help in the house. I'd like you to come back, Minya, as...housekeeper. If you would.'

Something flared in Minya's crinkled eyes. Before she could speak, Kate added quickly, 'I'm sure one of the stockmen's wives will lend a helping hand. And Tom, our current rouseabout, is there to do any heavy work— lifting, carrying in the firewood, and so forth. So you wouldn't have such a heavy workload as you had before.' Let Minya think that she blamed pressure of work for her unfortunate lapse.

'I never took that bracelet,' Minya said flatly. 'I ain't no thief.'

Kate flushed. 'Perhaps my husband...jumped to conclusions. Finding the necklace in your room.' Thinking quickly, she added soothingly, 'I'm sure it was all a mistake, Minya. In the flurry of my arrival, some- one must have picked it up and put it there, thinking it was yours.' But there had been only Jeremy, Minya and herself in the house! She hastened on, 'Please...put it out of your mind, Minya. I already have.' It was all in the past now, and not worth worrying about. Even at the time, she hadn't wanted Jeremy to dismiss Minya.

It had seemed far too harsh for a single misdemeanour. She had tentatively suggested that a scolding would suffice. But Jeremy had been adamant, and conscious already of the tension that existed between the two—undoubtedly due to Minya's special closeness to Nick—she had allowed her protests to subside.

'Nick's just come back for a visit?' Minya was frowning. 'He's not back for good?'

Kate hesitated. Would the woman refuse to come back if she thought that Nick's stay was only temporary?

'Nick wants to help me get the place back on its feet,' she answered carefully. 'He's taken on the job of overseer, now that Leif Clancy's gone.' She caught a relieved flicker in the old woman's eyes. 'So he's likely to be around for... a while.' But not for too long, she profoundly hoped. She'd be a fool to let him get too deeply entrenched in the place.

Perhaps she was being a fool letting him stay even temporarily. Why *was* she, knowing how dangerous he could be, knowing how much he must resent her presence here... his despised brother's widow?

She had no ready answer. She didn't even want to think about it. She just hoped that she wouldn't live to regret it.

She didn't wait around to watch Nick's reunion with Minya, leaving the kitchen the moment Nick appeared in the doorway, feeling they deserved that initial moment together, and waiting with Bernice and Ted until the two emerged later, arm in arm. Jeremy would have been calling her all kinds of fool, she reflected with a sigh, if he had been around to witness that cosy little twosome. She could almost hear his exasperated: 'Now you'll have the two of them plotting against you. What in heaven's name possessed you, Kate?' But whether it had been a

mistake or not, she felt lighter somehow. Despite her
qualms about what the future might hold, she felt she
had done the right thing in bringing Minya back to where
she belonged. Nick really had nothing to do with it. She
ought to have done it long ago.

Minya settled in as if she had never been away, happy
to have her beloved Nick home again. That night, after
Kate had taken her leave of Nick, who had already moved
his things into the overseer's house—of his own volition, and she hadn't tried to stop him, though she had
relented enough to invite him to share his evening meals
with her at the Big House—she found herself idly picking
up a photograph from the sideboard. A photograph of
Jeremy's mother Sophie. Nick's mother too, of course.
It was Sophie's wedding photograph, one of the few
photographs in the house.

She had been very beautiful—a dark-haired, dark-eyed
beauty...and Nick, Kate realised, looked so much like
her. They shared the same magnetic black eyes and
tumbled black hair, the same broad brow, the same
straight nose, the same wide, well shaped mouth. And
yet Jeremy had always described his half-brother as ugly,
swarthy, brooding...and she had assumed Nick must
have taken after his father. His real father, Kim, Logan
Ramsay's part-Aboriginal overseer, who had been so
tragically killed after fighting with Logan.

There were no photographs of Nick in the house—
not one. When Kate had remarked on it once to Jeremy,
he had told her that his father had removed every single
snapshot of Nick after he had banished Nick from the
house that final time. He hadn't wanted to be reminded
of the adopted son who had caused his family so much
pain. And yet, with this photograph of his wife Sophie

always on display, Logan must have been reminded of Nick every time he looked at it! Unless he had only had eyes for his beloved wife, and had managed to blot out the likeness between his wife and her younger son.

With a sigh, Kate replaced the photograph and turned away. If only she knew what Nick Ramsay was really up to, what he really had in mind...what he really *wanted*. A man like Nick was unlikely to be content to play second fiddle for long, that was for sure. Was she strong enough to hold out against him, to stand her ground until he finally gave up and left? Was that what she really wanted him to do? To leave?

She caught her breath, shocked that the question had even entered her head. She had a vision of Jeremy's horrified face, and felt a guilty flush sweep over her. Of course she wanted Nick to leave...the place wasn't big enough for both of them! And besides, he didn't deserve even a portion of it. He had forfeited his right to his old home long ago.

On the other hand...

She clamped her teeth down on her lip, trying to be brutally honest with herself. Once she had realised Jeremy's long-held dream and restored the property to its former prosperity, would she still want to stay on here—a young widow all alone, without a man, without a family, without close friends, with only her memories for company...and not always the happiest of memories? Once Nick Ramsay had finally given up and gone away for good, would she then consider selling up to somebody else and moving back to...?

Back to what?

Her heart constricted. She didn't even want to think about it. Not yet!

* * *

Nick settled into his position as overseer with almost frightening ease. His vast knowledge, his extensive experience, his commanding air of authority, and perhaps the fact that he was a Ramsay, and a very successful one at that, quickly earned the respect of the men, even the Aboriginal stockmen, who had always seemed rather surly with Jeremy, and at times with Kate too, though, in view of Nick's natural heritage and his family link with Minya, perhaps it wasn't so surprising. On the other hand, Nick was first and foremost a Ramsay, with all the privileges that name entailed, and he wouldn't have earned their respect lightly. Nick managed, within days, and without causing any friction among the men, to sort out which ones were pulling their weight and which ones they could best afford to let go.

His skills on a horse, Kate found, equalled his skills at the controls of his plane. Like Jeremy, he was a superb natural horseman—he not only looked good in the saddle, he could handle any situation with consummate ease, from rounding up the wildest cattle to breaking in a savagely bucking horse.

With her agreement he had stronger stockyards built, organised new fencing where needed, saw to the repair and repainting of the gates and made suggestions for upgrading the stock. Sometimes Kate found herself wondering with vague disquiet who the true boss was here—she or her new temporary overseer. But as long as she could see the property improving—and it was, in leaps and bounds—she was prepared to let Nick have his head...at least for the time being, and as long as the improvements he made were within her means. There would come a time, she knew, when one of them would have to give in and go...but she was determined that, when that day came, it was not going to be her. Certainly

not if it meant handing the place over to Nick—
Dominic—Ramsay. Later perhaps, if another buyer came
along, one who had no link with her brother-in-
law... then she would see.

One evening, after they had been going through the
books together in the homestead office, Nick suggested
introducing a computerised system of book-keeping,
which he said would save Kate hours of work. When she
protested about the cost, and the time it would take to
set it up, he waved aside her objections.

'My business in Sydney has just installed new com-
puters, and there are some old ones going begging. I'll
have one sent out—it won't cost you a thing. We've been
giving them away to anyone who wants one. I'll help
you set it up myself.'

As he bent over her from behind she could feel the
fine hairs at her nape rising in response to his nearness,
and she hated herself for it. She couldn't understand how
her body's reaction to this man—her husband's bitterest
enemy—could be so far removed from the way her conscious mind was telling her she ought to react. She only
hoped *he* wasn't aware of it.

To be on the safe side, she found herself scrupulously
avoiding any physical contact with him over the following days, even taking pains to avoid meeting him eye
to eye. But that wasn't such a good idea either, because
she suspected after a while that he was beginning to
wonder *why* she was being so evasive. To compensate,
she was often sharper with him than she might otherwise
have been, and it inflamed her when he seemed more
amused than put out.

The sooner he realises I'm not going to pack it in and
go, she brooded, irked as much by his infuriating calm

as by her own inexplicable response to him, the sooner
he'll grow tired of waiting, of pouring his energies into
a lost cause . . . and then he'll give up and go away, and
I'll be rid of him. And that moment can't be too soon
for me!

Jeremy had always been immensely proud of his polo
ponies, and Kate hadn't had the heart to sell them, or
even think of selling them, even though they meant a
lot of extra hard work and expense. She had decided to
go on tending and breeding the ponies, knowing that
was what Jeremy would have wanted. Jeremy's ponies
had always been magnificent animals, widely admired,
and any he sold had always fetched a good price.

But they were a handful, she couldn't deny it. Even
Jeremy had spent rather too much time with them, she
had secretly, treacherously, thought at times. There were
so many other things on a busy cattle station that needed
attending to, or money spent on.

She stood watching Jeremy's prize chestnut, Glory,
rolling in the sand-roll, admiring the pony's sleek flanks,
her proud head, her long slender legs. What a beauty
she was! As the mare thrashed about in the sand, Kate
noticed with a gasp of horror that the pony had prised
loose a shoe. Knowing that a protruding piece of steel
horseshoe could cut like a knife, she jumped into the
sand-roll without a second thought and pulled the loose
shoe from Glory's flailing leg—mercifully before any
damage was done.

As she staggered back, breathing hard, she felt a hand
touch her arm. A tremor ran through her, even before
she twisted her head round to see Nick Ramsay towering
over her. She caught a flare of surprise in his eyes, and
something else that made her heart give a strange little

flip. And then she recovered her senses and said with a shrug, dismissing the incident, 'I thought she might cut herself.'

'She might have cut *you*,' Nick said softly, and she let her gaze flutter away from his, trying not to be affected by the unaccustomed warmth she had glimpsed in his eyes—only to find her gaze transfixed to the rich outline of his shoulders straining against his shirt. She gave herself a mental shake, and realising that his hand was still on her arm and that he must surely have felt the tremor that ran through her at his touch—she hoped he would put it down to reaction at the dangerous situation she had only just managed to avert—she hastily stepped away, deliberately withdrawing her arm from his grasp.

'One learns to react quickly,' she said with studied nonchalance, as if she faced situations like that every day. 'What are you doing here, anyway? I thought you were overseeing the drafting and branding.' She heard the abrasiveness in her voice, and knew it was unwarranted, but it was better than showing the weakness that for some reason he so often made her feel. Weakness at a touch, weakness at a mere glance...it was crazy! Not even Jeremy had sent tremors through her at a mere touch, a mere look. That it should be *Nick Ramsay* of all men who was capable of affecting her this way...the last man on earth she would ever...

'We've just about finished.' Nick's voice cut into her thoughts, his tone curt now, businesslike, and despite herself she felt a strange little tug as she saw the warmth fade from his eyes. 'Kate, we need to talk about the polo ponies.'

She went still. 'What about them?' she asked, frowning. Did he want to take them over too?

'I think it's time you got rid of them,' he said bluntly. 'Looking after them is taking up too much time and energy... and draining the property of money we should be using elsewhere. If you sell now, while they're in peak condition, they should fetch a top price.'

Kate's eyes dilated, green pools of distress. 'No, I can't! I'd never...' Those polo ponies had been Jeremy's pride and joy. He had devoted hours to them... grooming, breeding, exercising, tending. He had loved them with a passion, treasured them. There had even been times, in those final months of their life together, when she had wondered, poignantly, if he loved his polo ponies more than he had loved her!

'Be realistic, Kate. You don't play polo, and neither do I or anyone else here at Ramsay Downs. We'd be better off buying some new stock horses—horses we can use, to work on the property. A good stock horse isn't expensive!'

Kate drew in a fractured breath, her hand fluttering up to brush her hair from her eyes. The suggestion made sense—she couldn't deny it. But she would feel disloyal to Jeremy even considering it. His beloved polo ponies! His greatest joy. In the last months of his life, perhaps his *only* joy. His joy and his consolation.

'I'll think about it,' was as far as she would go. Nick Ramsay has no heart, no sentiment, she thought. Only cold, heartless logic. And yet she couldn't deny that what he said was right... the right thing for Ramsay Downs. They had to cut down where they could if they were to survive, let alone see the station expand and flourish.

But Nick wasn't satisfied with just thinking about it. 'I wouldn't leave it too long, Kate. I'd sell while they're at their peak. Want me to make some enquiries?'

He was hassling her, but... She spread her hands. 'I don't know... it seems such a waste.' She turned away to watch Glory shaking herself of sand. Such a magnificent animal! No wonder she had been her husband's favourite. 'Jeremy spent hours on those horses. They were his pride and joy,' she said in a muffled voice. 'How could I——?'

Nick lost patience with her. 'Maybe if he'd spent less time pampering his ponies, the place wouldn't be in such a mess now!'

She paled, and he at once caught her arm, his face stricken with remorse. 'I'm sorry, Kate, I shouldn't have said that. I don't hold it against Jeremy, believe me. Everyone is entitled to an interest, a special pastime. But he's gone now, Kate, and we don't need his polo ponies any more. We need to look to the future.'

She shook off his hand the second he touched her, noting his use of 'we', not 'you'. 'Whose future are you talking about?' she asked, resentment throbbing through her voice. 'Mine... or *yours*?'

'Can't it be *ours*, Kate? Yours *and* mine? Let me buy into it—share it with you. Equal partners.'

She jerked back, away from him. 'And just what sort of partnership do you have in mind? You're hoping I won't stay here, aren't you? You want me to leave! And then you'd have the place all to yourself!'

'I'm thinking of both our futures, Kate,' he said, sidestepping her question. 'It's true, I do want to buy Ramsay Downs. I want to see it as it used to be—bigger and better, in fact. And I'm willing to buy it outright, at a price you wouldn't get from anyone else. But if you don't want to sell, Kate, then let me buy *into* it. Become your partner.'

Her eyes narrowed. 'You wouldn't want to share Ramsay Downs with me!' Or I with you, she added silently. Jeremy would turn in his grave at the very thought. After what Nick Ramsay had done to Jeremy over the years, he didn't deserve a share.

'On the contrary, I'd be perfectly happy to let you retain a half-share in the property, Kate. You could come and visit whenever you liked—to make sure that I'm looking after the place properly.'

She blanched. 'You *do* want me to leave!'

'I think it would be best, Kate. Best for you.'

Fury whipped through her. 'Best for *you*, you mean!'

'Best for both of us,' he conceded. 'Even better, perhaps, if you sold the place outright. Made a clean break.'

She was speechless. A clean break...so that they never needed to see each other again! Did he hate her that much? Unconsciously she pressed her hand to her throat. Of course he hated her. She had been Jeremy's wife. And he had hated and resented Jeremy all the days of his life, hated him enough to go to any lengths to discredit him, and worse. No wonder he didn't want Jeremy's wife around as a constant reminder of his black past!

'Look, Kate, this is no place for a woman like you...a beautiful young woman on your own, without even a family to grow up and take over from you one day.' Nick's voice went on, low, gently persuasive. 'Don't bury yourself out here. You can't go on mourning Jeremy forever. Let go of him...it's time you cut the cable and made a new life for yourself.'

She stared at him, resentment darkening her eyes. How like her parents he sounded! But there was one very big difference. She could take it from them, knowing they had her own interests at heart. But Nick Ramsay was thinking only of himself. Of what he wanted.

'What about your own life?' she flashed back. 'You have no wife, no family, no ties. Why would *you* want to bury yourself here? And how long would you stay? You're forever taking on jobs overseas!'

'I've finished with my work overseas,' he said, and added simply, 'I want a place I can call home. Ramsay Downs has always been my home, so it's natural I'd want to settle down here.'

'You have other properties... surely you could settle down on one of those?' Kate cast around for further arguments. 'And you have your business interests in Sydney... you could make a home for yourself there, in the city.'

He gave a wry smile. 'I have no wish to live in the city. I can always visit when I need to conduct business there. My company doesn't need my constant presence— I pay good men good money to run it for me. And as for my other properties, they have no special significance to me, on a personal level. And they're in perfectly good hands.'

As if realising he was being side-tracked, he gave a slight frown, and went back on the attack. 'Go back to where you belong, Kate. This is a harsh world out here...it's not for a young woman on her own. A woman like you, Kate...you need more out of life. You need close friends, company, comforts...perhaps, in time, even a new man in your life.'

She recoiled...not so much at the thought of a new man in her life, but with guilt, because only moments ago she had found herself already reacting to another man...the last man on earth she ought to be reacting to! Was it simply loneliness? Proximity? The fact that she and Jeremy, in their last weeks together, hadn't...

She sighed. No, she thought heavily, with a despondent shake of her head. If it was just a man she wanted—*any* man—there were plenty of available men around here beside Nick Ramsay that she could have...

'Kate, I'm aware there are some women who do manage to battle on alone in the outback...' The persuasive voice wasn't letting up. 'But it's hard, Kate—the climate, the tough daily grind, keeping the men in order... It hardens a woman, adds years to her looks...' He seized both of her hands and turned them over, palms down. 'Such pretty hands! But how long do you think they'll stay soft and smooth and unblemished? Think what the fierce sun and the wind and the dust will do to them, and to that lovely face of yours, in time...' His gaze, darkly compelling, flickered up again to meet hers. 'Imagine how that gentle, refined voice of yours will roughen after months, years of shouting at the men to assert your control over them. Don't let it happen, Kate...go back home where you belong. You need more out of life than you'll find out here...a young woman, all alone.'

He was stroking her hands with his fingers as he spoke, and, incensed as she was, much as she wanted to snatch them away, his touch was having a strangely hypnotic effect on her, mesmerising her, paralysing her where she stood. As Nick stood over her, breathlessly close, she felt her anger warring with something else, something she couldn't comprehend, that made no sense. Her heart was hammering, her breathing ragged, and it was only with a supreme effort that she managed to find her voice, a thin sound, quite unlike her own.

'I have all I want right here. I have enough to satisfy me for years.'

The seductive stroking didn't falter. 'Have you, Kate?' The black glitter of his gaze, vibrantly masculine, flared over her, making her acutely aware of herself as a woman—and worse, far worse, of him as a man. Heat raced along her veins, every nerve end in her body leaping with treacherous anticipation.

'It'll be lonely, Kate. You really think you'll have enough here to satisfy you?' he asked softly. She felt his fingers close over hers, felt them tightening, pulling her closer, closer, until her hands were crushed against the hard wall of his chest. She felt a breathless tension, and couldn't move, couldn't speak.

'You honestly expect me to believe you don't need a man, Kate?' he murmured, his tanned face swimming over hers, his warm breath fanning her cheek. 'Your body tells me something different. I can feel it...I can feel you trembling...' His fingers felt for the pulse at her wrist. 'My, how it's racing!'

Her eyes widened, emerald pools of stricken dismay. She tried to jerk away from him then, appalled at what her body must be giving away, only to feel his fingers tighten on her wrist.

Resorting to anger, she flashed him a look of disdain. 'You're crazy!' she cried huskily. 'If I'm trembling, it's because you're making me so—so mad. Let go of me! You're hurting me!'

'Sorry.' But he didn't slacken his grip. He laughed softly, mockingly. 'What are you afraid of, Kate?'

'Not *you*. I don't need anyone...and if I did, it would never be you. *Never*! Not if you were the last man on earth!'

A tiny red flame flickered in the night-black eyes. 'No?' he challenged, and, with one hand still firmly clasping hers, he slid his other round her tense body, his fingers digging into her spine through the thin layer of her shirt, burning into the soft flesh underneath.

Her heart began pounding as if she had been running up a steep hill, and heat rushed to her face as the black eyes scorched hers, as if he were wickedly aware of the build-up of tension that she was trying desperately to control.

'No!' The denial exploded from her lips. At the same time a trembling anger bubbled inside her. She didn't want his hands on her; she didn't want him touching her. It gave her a feeling she had never felt before, not even with Jeremy—the feeling that she was no longer in control. She didn't want to feel like this—especially not here, not now, and least of all with this man of all men!

She tried desperately to tear herself away, but his grip was implacable, allowing her only enough room to lean back, away from him. Knowing her physical strength was no match for his, she lashed out at him with her tongue, blindly, with a desperation she couldn't hide.

'Let me go! I hate you touching me—I *hate* it!'

Hearing in dismay the tremor in her voice, she began to abuse him, mortified at the way he was making her feel, hating him, wanting to hurt him as much as she had ever wanted to hurt anyone in her life.

'Do you think I don't know all about you...what you're capable of...what you've done to your brother over the years? You don't deserve to be allowed to set one foot on Ramsay land! You're a disgrace to your family name!'

She flinched away from him as she felt his body tense, raw fury blazing in the depthless black eyes. She thought for a second that he was going to strike her.

Instead, he jerked her savagely towards him and clamped his mouth down on hers, cutting off her gasp of protest in a searing, punishing kiss that made her heart seize up in panic. The pressure of his lips was implacable, giving her no chance to struggle free, and, realising she was helpless, she went rigid under the assault. Fury, resentment, and a helpless despair were warring inside her, spiced with an inexplicable mixture of fear and excitement, and other emotions she couldn't even begin to define.

With cynical expertise Nick teased her tight lips apart, demanding a response that she was determined not to give. But to her dismay she felt her lips stir under his in a response of their own that she was totally unable to control. Slight though the movement was, he felt it, and his kiss changed and deepened, his mouth moving over hers until she felt boneless, liquefied, her senses spinning.

For a long, agonising minute his mouth held hers, then he raised his head a fraction and she opened dazed eyes. For a second they stared at each other, and she saw in the jet-black eyes tiny golden flecks around the pupil she had never noticed before. And then he thrust her savagely away from him, drawing a deep ragged breath.

'It was either kiss you,' he grated, 'or wring your neck!'

She tottered back, clutching at the air with a trembling hand, just managing to steady herself as his hand shot out to give her support. She leapt back, away from him, recoiling as if stung.

'You—you——' Words failed her.

'Face it, Kate,' Nick's voice roughened, 'you're vulnerable, here on your own. I've just proved it to you. Leif Clancy was another case in point.'

She gasped, her face hot with humiliation. 'I—I hate you!' Her breath burned in her throat, a choking anger taking over at the memory of his kiss, and what had prompted it. 'I have no intention of selling Ramsay Downs,' she ground out, her eyes throwing out green sparks. 'Now or ever. Least of all to you!'

She saw a shadow of annoyance cross his face—perhaps partly directed at himself, for going too far, for goading her. He masked it quickly.

'You're letting the past cloud your judgement, Kate. Be practical. You've seen what I can do for this place. Look ahead, Kate, not back. Can't we bury the past?'

She faced him, hands clenched into tight fists. 'I *was* looking ahead—until you turned up and brought the past rushing back.'

His brow darkened, his eyes fierce, black as night, his chest heaving, then falling as he expelled a long slow breath. 'Look...' He managed to curb his anger, his tone tightly restrained now, cautious. 'If you're adamant about not wanting to sell, then consider my offer of a partnership. You can come and go as you please. You can have the best of both worlds.'

Her eyes narrowed, clawing him like talons. He thought—*hoped*—that once she went back home, once she made some friends, or met another man, she wouldn't come back. Wouldn't *want* to come back.

'And what if I do meet another man?' she challenged, throwing back her head, causing waves of silky gold hair to ripple in the sunlight. 'A man who loves the outback as much as I do, and wants to bring me back to Ramsay

Downs to live. What would you do then, Nick Ramsay? I don't think the place would be big enough for both of us—for all three of us!'

He glowered at her, his eyes like black, hot coal. He hadn't considered that she might want to come back one day—with a new husband!

'Then I'd leave,' he said after a long pause. 'I'd sell back my share—or part of it. I'm sure you wouldn't miss the small corner of land in the far north-west.'

Kate's eyes flew to his. 'Why?' she asked sharply. 'That area's not suitable for grazing . . . it's arid country, with deep ravines and hills. Quite useless for stock!'

'Then you wouldn't miss it, would you?'

'Why would *you* want it?' she demanded, a growing suspicion uncoiling inside her.

He shrugged. 'It's Aboriginal land. My grandfather—Kim's father—was born there, in one of the caves there. It's where my roots are.'

She kept her eyes on his face, scepticism heavy in the look she gave him. For a man apparently so lacking in sentiment, he was being uncharacteristically sentimental. It simply didn't ring true. Especially in view of what she knew of that particular region . . . Did *he* know? she wondered, mistrust puckering her brow. As a Ramsay, he must be aware of the old family rumour, but did he have any idea that there was real substance to it? No, how could he? He couldn't possibly know what Jeremy had recently stumbled on in that remote region. Jeremy had kept quiet about it, telling only her, and swearing her to secrecy—and, sadly, he had died before he'd had a chance to do anything further about it. As for herself, she had had so much else to think about since she had been left on her own that she hadn't given it another thought...until now.

All she knew was that Nick Ramsay must never find out what Jeremy had discovered there. Jeremy had warned her of the consequences—to him, to her, to their safety and well-being—if his ruthless brother ever found out. Somehow she had to turn Nick against the area—and quickly!

'I wouldn't have thought that you—a Ramsay—would be sentimental about such a tragic place,' she threw back at him. 'Jeremy said that his father—Logan Ramsay—always avoided the area like the plague, and insisted that his family shun it too, because his father was killed there...by the Aborigines!'

She caught a faint flicker in the narrowed black eyes. Nick was obviously aware of the tragedy. No doubt he also knew what had lured Logan's father to the area in the first place. But did he give the old man's quest any credence? It had been kept a closely guarded family secret, and over the years the ill-fated venture had sunk into the realm of legend, no one being prepared, at least during Logan Ramsay's lifetime, to take the risk of finding out for sure if the old man's dream had held any real substance.

'Have *you* ever been there?' asked Nick, and, though his tone was impassive, giving nothing away, there was a watchfulness in his eye that seemed to bely the carelessness of the question.

'No, I haven't,' she answered truthfully, adding in a tone as impassive as his, 'It's a dreary, remote place, from what I've heard. Why would anyone want to go there?'

Nick jerked a shoulder. 'I just thought you might have been curious to see where . . . Logan's father was killed. I thought Jeremy might have taken you there.'

She gave a mock shudder. 'No, thanks! Too gruesome for me.'

His eyes seemed to narrow further, piercing hers with a knife-edge of glinting ebony, as if he were looking for a sign that she knew more than she was saying. She resolved to go on the attack.

'Why would *you* want that piece of land? Wouldn't it be a constant reminder of what your forebears did to Logan Ramsay's father, an innocent station-owner? Who also happened to be your adopted grandfather!'

'Innocent?' Nick seized on the word, echoing it derisively. 'The Aborigines considered it their land, not his. Sacred Aboriginal land. To them, *he* was the interloper.'

'But to kill him . . . for no reason!'

'No reason? Isn't it more likely that they saw him as threatening their existence in some way?'

'In *what* way?' she demanded. If Nick knew what Logan's father had gone there to look for, or what he planned to do if he found it, let him spell it out!

'Look, they were merely protecting what they considered their own.'

He wasn't going to admit it, even if he did know. Not to *her*—Jeremy's widow. Kate turned away with a frustrated sigh. If Nick Ramsay wanted that arid north-west region for the same reason Jeremy had wanted it, it was obvious he was going to keep it to himself. As for herself, she had no intention of letting Nick Ramsay lay a finger on that remote corner, valuable or not, or any other part of Ramsay Downs. He didn't deserve it. For what he had done to Jeremy in the past, he had forfeited any right to it for all time.

She owed it to Jeremy—and to Logan Ramsay too—to keep Ramsay Downs safely out of Dominic Ramsay's rapacious clutches.

CHAPTER FOUR

THE Cessna flew low over Logan's Plain, which made up much of the northern part of the station. It was prime country—coolibah country—which had never needed clearing. In the distance a row of trees marked the fence line, the trees so far away that they were no more than a smudgy green line shimmering in the heat.

Kate had decided to come with Nick while he flew out to check the fences around the north paddock. It gave her a chance to inspect the station from the air, a task that normally took days in a four-wheel-drive. At the same time it gave her a chance to keep a wary eye on Nick, on where he was and what he was doing while he was so far from the homestead.

The Cessna swooped low as they reached the fenceline, and Nick's eyes narrowed in concentration. Kate leaned forward too, following his gaze, and for some time neither spoke, both intent on the job at hand.

When they had covered the area to their satisfaction, Nick sat back and shouted over the drone of the engine, 'A pity all the property isn't like this. It's real Texas country... ideal for cattle. Especially those fellows.' He inclined his head in the direction of the white hump-backed Brahmans and cherry-red Santa Gertrudis cattle grazing below. Being hardy creatures, resistant to heat and disease, they thrived in these conditions.

Kate tensed, hearing only the words, '*A pity all the property isn't like this.*' Was he thinking of the arid corner in the remote north-west? Surely he wasn't heading in that direction!

'I'll show you what I mean,' said Nick, adding, 'There's a suggestion I want to make.'

The plane was gaining height, banking gently, but no, Kate realised in relief, they weren't heading north-west. They were heading east. Within minutes they were flying over the section of the property that consisted of heavy gidgee and brigalow scrub, so prolific that it was almost a jungle. Thousands of acres of it.

Nick jerked his head sideways. 'That mass of scrub down there is what's keeping your stocking rate low. If it could be cleared, even in part, you'd see a dramatic improvement.'

Kate frowned, pursing her lips. 'It would cost too much,' she said with a shake of her head. It would be far beyond her modest means, at any rate. And even if she did manage to raise the money, there was no certainty that the huge investment would ever be repaid. She voiced her argument aloud. 'Even if I could find the money to clear it,' she said tightly, 'regrowth of the scrub after it had been cleared would be certain to be a problem. And the cost of keeping it cleared could go on for years. It would cost a fortune!'

'You could clear a few hundred acres at a time, not all at once,' Nick said, and went on to describe how it could be done. 'Let me provide the capital, Kate. A loan,' he added quickly, as she turned sharply to face him.

'No,' she said flatly.

'Just a loan, Kate. An interest-free loan, without conditions. No time limit on repayment. You would still retain full ownership of Ramsay Downs.'

'Why would you make an offer like that?' she gasped. 'What would you get out of it?'

'I'm confident that the investment would pay off, that you'd have no problem repaying the loan eventually. Even if you couldn't, I'm willing to take the risk. I want to see Ramsay Downs thrive, even if I...don't end up staying here. It's the least I can do for my old home—for my brother's widow. Well, Kate, what do you think?'

She found herself hesitating. Impressed as she had been so far with the way Nick was running the property and with the way he handled the men, and even, grudgingly, for the ideas he had put up for improving the station, she had refused, so far, to let him inject any of his own money into the property, afraid that it might rebound on her later, and put her under too much of an obligation to him.

But a loan... An *unconditional* loan...

Noting her indecision, Nick pressed home his point. 'You've nothing to lose, Kate. Look, I know you think I've done some less than admirable things in the past,' he said, his voice a low rumble over the whine of the Cessna's engine, 'and I know you think I don't deserve one square acre of Ramsay Downs. But haven't you considered the possibility that I might want to...make amends for the past? That I might be a changed man? You'd be cutting off your nose to spite your face if you didn't let me do at least this much for the property.'

She stared unseeingly at the forest below, her hands clasped tightly in her lap. What if what he said was true, and he really had changed? Why shouldn't she let him do something substantial for the station—he certainly owed it something, after the unforgivable things he had done in the past. And she knew he could afford it. Perhaps he truly did regret what he had done, and was genuinely trying to make amends, genuinely trying to help her build the place up again, without expecting anything in return. Perhaps she had been too hard on him . . .

On the other hand—she winced as she felt her fingernails biting into her flesh—what if this was simply a clever ruse to get her to let down her guard? What if he had decided that this was the best way to drive her out eventually . . . to appear to be helping her, to appear to be her friend, with all the old enmity behind them . . . ?

'Look, I know what you think of me, Kate.' Nick leaned sideways, his mouth close to her ear, his voice softly seductive. 'I know you don't trust me, that you think I want to take Ramsay Downs away from you. But if you're determined to stay on here, and go on running the place yourself, then I'll bow to your decision . . . and still do everything I can to help you. I'll stay until the place is the way you want it to be, and then, if you still want to stay on here, I'll do as I said I would and go. No strings attached. Deal?'

She stirred uneasily in her seat. Could she trust him? Dared she trust him? This was a complete about-face. The Nick Ramsays of this world never backed down, never gave in. Jeremy, if he were here, would be warning her to take care, not to trust a word he said.

Would he really simply pack up and leave, once the place was back on its feet and she had convinced him that she still wanted to stay? Why did the thought of him leaving cause a ripple of disquiet, almost a sinking feeling inside her? It was what she wanted . . . there was no question about that. And yet it *was* difficult running the place on her own—she'd be stupid to deny it. And Nick was doing a superb job as overseer. He was so much more reliable, more far-seeing, more experienced than Leif Clancy had ever been.

She drew in a deep, tremulous breath. It couldn't be that she was coming to depend on Nick...that would be fatal! No doubt that was what he was secretly relying on...that she would be so impressed by what he was doing for the place that in the end she would overlook what he had done in the past and ask him to stay on, to take over the place entirely, and then bow out herself, knowing she would be leaving the property in good hands!

She compressed her lips. How *could* she ever overlook what he had done to Jeremy? She couldn't...she mustn't! One thing she was very sure of—the place would never be big enough for both of them, not on a permanent basis. There were too many skeletons, too many painful memories—his very presence would be a perpetual reminder. And she would never be able to feel that she could entirely trust him.

As for Nick—if he had any conscience at all, neither would he want *her* anywhere around *him*. She would be a constant thorn in his side, a constant reminder to him of what he had done to her husband in the past.

'Well, Kate, what do you say?'

She started, her eyes snapping round. 'Oh. Sure. Maybe.' Whatever happened in the future, why not, in the meantime, go on making use of Nick's expertise and his services—and even his money, if it was offered in such a way that it didn't give him any control over her, or over the property? He owed Ramsay Downs some reparation for his past misdemeanours. And as long as she kept her head and didn't let him gain a permanent foothold here, or undermine her authority, what did she have to lose?

*   *   *

'That looks like the Stantons' Range Rover,' Nick commented as they drove back to the homestead from the airstrip. The vehicle was parked in front of the Big House, in the shade of a giant bottle tree.

Minya emerged from the house. 'You got a visitor,' she said in her raspy voice. 'She's round by the pool.' Contented as she had been since she had been back at Ramsay Downs, careful not to put a foot wrong, Minya rarely unbent so far as to openly smile at Kate. But that was partly her nature, Kate was learning, and she tried not to take it to heart.

'You mean...it's Bernice?' she asked in surprise. Bernice hated driving in the outback. On the few occasions she had come to visit, Ted had flown her over in his Piper Cherokee.

Minya's screwed-up eyes glinted in the afternoon sunlight. 'Not her—her daughter. Abigail.'

Kate drew in a quick breath. *Abigail* was here? Unconsciously she reached up to smooth her hair.

'Well, well, so Abby's back!' drawled Nick, and Kate shot him a look from under her wide-brimmed hat. But his tanned face was as usual an impassive mask, giving nothing away. What did *he* think of his former sister-in-law? she wondered, searching his closed face, in vain, for a clue. Growing up as neighbours, they must have known each other reasonably well—and, from memory, they would be somewhere around the same age, early thirties.

'Nick!'

A bronzed willowy figure in a brief white bikini burst from the shrubbery at the side of the house, tanned arms outstretched, glowing auburn curls bouncing. As the girl hurled herself at Nick, his face broke into a smile and he grabbed her in a warm embrace. Witnessing the exuberant reunion, Kate felt a quiver of unease. The two made a fine-looking couple ... and they were obviously old friends, good friends. And here they were, both back on their home territory, both free and unencumbered, both looking perhaps to settle down ...

Not here, you won't! Kate thought vehemently. If you want to settle down together, you can settle down at Doon-gara, not here. She took a quick step forward.

'I'm Kate Ramsay,' she said a trifle too forcefully, and held her breath as the couple drew apart at last. Abigail swung her head round, her red lips curving into a faintly ironic smile.

'So...you're Mrs Jeremy Ramsay the second,' she said, her voice a deep amused drawl. Her eyes were an unusual amber shade, Kate noticed, and were openly speculative as they swept over her, taking in every detail. Kate found herself doing the same, noting the girl's stunning bone structure, the proud sweep of her chin, the way her rich auburn hair curled over her ivory-smooth brow, which, unlike her tanned limbs, looked as if it had never been exposed to the sun. Jeremy had never told her that his first wife was such a beauty.

For her part, Abigail was absorbing the delicate oval of Kate's gently tanned face, the clear green eyes under the wide brow, the generous mouth, the slender grace of her figure, and as the girl made her appraisal Kate saw her quite visibly stiffen, something in the cool amber eyes appearing to harden. Kate stopped breathing, wondering if the girl saw her as competition. If only she knew!

'I hope you don't mind me inviting myself to dinner,' Abigail said, so airily that Kate wondered if she had imagined the girl's reaction. 'I did ring before I came, but you'd already left. Minya told me you'd be back by late afternoon, so I had a leisurely drive here and arrived about half an hour ago. I've been making use of the pool. I'd forgotten how damned hot it gets out in these parts.'

'I'm glad you did,' said Kate, injecting warmth into her voice. If they were going to be neighbours, it would be much easier if they could be friends. 'The pool can be a real lifesaver,' she agreed. When she had first come to Ramsay Downs the pool had been in a state of neglect, and it had been one of the promised improvements that Jeremy had given top priority, knowing she wasn't used to the outback heat. In those days he had been so enthusiastic, so eager to please, and everything had been so perfect, so full of... hope.

'You won't mind putting me up for the night as well, will you?' Abigail asked carelessly. 'By the time we've had dinner it'll be too late to drive all the way back. It's too dangerous driving at night—the 'roos can be lethal in the dark.'

'Of course you must stay,' said Kate, mentally thanking her lucky stars that Nick had moved out of the Big House. If Abigail had any thoughts of ensnaring Nick Ramsay, she wouldn't take kindly to hearing that Nick and Jeremy's young widow were living under the same roof. As it was, Nick's quarters were only a few steps from the Big House, across the yard. Quite handy enough for Abigail to visit *him* secretly later on, if she so wished.

Would Nick welcome a nocturnal visit from his old childhood friend? Kate pondered idly, and with the thought came a slight pang. She dismissed it at once, mentally explaining it away: It's just the thought of them both getting together... plotting together... against *me*. Just another thing to worry about! If it's not Nick and

Minya, it's Nick and Abigail. Who do I have on my side? she pondered gloomily. Not a soul! Even her own men were already relating more closely to Nick than they ever had to her. Not that she could entirely blame them. She was a woman, after all, which must make it difficult for them, and she was the owner of the station—the big boss—and it was the overseer's job, not hers so much, to relate directly to the men.

'I'd better go and check on what's been going on here,' Nick put in, tilting his hat back with one hand and thrusting the thumb of his other hand into his leather belt, in that easy masculine way of his that made him look so much a part of the outback. 'Then I'll change and join you both for a drink before dinner.'

'Wonderful!' cried Abigail, and Kate nodded, smiling faintly, wondering, not for the first time, who was calling the shots here, she or her autocratic overseer.

Left alone with Abigail, she felt a sudden awkwardness, wondering if the girl resented her—the second wife, the younger woman, who, after a marriage lasting less than two years, had inherited all this.

'I guess you'd like to go in and change too?' she asked pleasantly, flicking her gaze over the girl's skimpy bikini.

'In a minute. Come with me while I fetch my towel.' Abigail moved forward with animal grace, showing no sign of self-consciousness. She shot a look over her shoulder at Kate and murmured, with a faint undercurrent of dryness, 'So you're still in mourning for Jeremy.'

'What... do you mean?' Kate glanced down at her white shirt and blue denim jeans—hardly mourning gear.

The girl gave a short laugh. 'Oh, mourning doesn't have to be wearing black and staying behind closed doors. I mean the fact that you're still here, at Ramsay

Downs, hiding yourself away from the world. That's not good, for a young woman all alone.'

Not another one! Kate thought, stifling a sigh. 'Ramsay Downs is my home,' she said levelly. 'I'm not hiding myself away. And I'm not lonely,' she added for good measure.

The girl tilted her head, her amber eyes narrowing, impaling hers. 'From what I hear, you're a city girl, Kate. Why would you want to stay on here now that Jeremy's gone? This land can't mean anything to you.'

The direct approach. Kate held on to her temper. 'It does mean a lot to me, actually. And it meant everything to my husband. He had great plans for Ramsay Downs— we both did. I intend to see them through. It was Jeremy's dream to... restore the place to the way it used to be.'

'Jeremy's *dream*?' Abigail gave an undignified snort. 'You fell for that, Kate? Jeremy never cared about Ramsay Downs. He only cared about himself, and his polo ponies, and scoring over Nick. And above all, keeping Ramsay Downs out of Nick's hands. He hated his brother more than he loved Ramsay Downs. Why do you think he married *you*?'

Kate caught her breath. 'What—what do you mean?'

'Oh, Kate, don't tell me you never suspected! He felt he had to marry to cut his brother out. He knew that if anything happened to him—if he died unmarried and without a family to inherit after him—Ramsay Downs would have gone straight to Nick.'

Kate felt a curious lightheadedness, as if the blood had drained from her face. 'Don't be ridiculous! Such a thing would never have entered his——'

'No? You must be familiar with the terms of his father's will, Kate. Logan Ramsay left the station to

Jeremy—sure. As he was the oldest son, and his only natural son, that was only logical. But Logan's will also decreed that if Jeremy died without leaving a wife or a family, Nick was to inherit the property.'

Kate brow puckered. 'Well, that only makes sense. It was simply a precaution...to cut out a lot of red tape, in the unlikely event that—that——'

'Yes, dear, maybe so. But remember, I was married to Jeremy too once. I know how his mind worked—and, believe me, the thought of Ramsay Downs going to Nick one day—or *Dominic*, as he persisted in calling him—constantly preyed on his mind. He hoped that he and I would have children...lots of children...to ensure that Nick would be cut out for good. And when I failed to conceive, and when a specialist told us I could never have children, that was it. End of marriage!'

Kate gave a tiny gasp. 'You're saying...your marriage failed because you couldn't have a *child*?'

'That's right.' Veering off the path, Abigail bent down with fluid elegance to retrieve her towel and sandals. 'Jeremy bowed out, quicker than a speeding bullet!'

Kate shook her head disbelievingly. 'But—but he told me you split up because you'd realised you weren't suited. He never even mentioned children.'

'Well, no, he wouldn't, would he?' The girl straightened, her red lips twisting. 'Sounds positively feudal, doesn't it, a man giving his poor wife the flick simply because she can't give him a son? The ironic part is, I went to a different specialist later on, and found that I only needed a slight operation to make me as good as new. So the last laugh was on Jeremy! He should have stuck around. Oh, don't look so mortified, Kate...I doubt if the marriage would have lasted anyway. We *weren't* suited, as it happens. And I was never crazy about having kids.'

As Kate stood awkwardly, at a loss to know what to say, Abigail nonchalantly flicked her towel round her smooth golden shoulders and said, 'When I heard that Jeremy had married again a couple of years ago, I wasn't surprised that he'd chosen someone so much younger the second time around. A hale and healthy, robust young show-jumper...presumably highly fertile,' she added drily. 'He must have been devastated when you failed to produce a child as well.'

Kate winced. 'Any husband would be upset. We were *both* upset—we both longed for a family. You make it sound as if he only wanted——'

'Look, I'm sorry, Kate,' Abigail cut in, reaching out to touch her arm with a cool hand. 'I realise it must have been painful to you too. But I *knew* Jeremy. I was married to him too, remember. And we were alike in many ways. We both knew what we wanted and went after it, singlemindedly. Two of a kind, you might say. That gave us a kind of chemistry—in the beginning, at least. It soon fizzled out when he knew I couldn't have his child. Did he send you to a specialist too?' she asked curiously.

Kate flushed, and didn't answer. Would Jeremy have walked out on her too, she wondered heavily, if she, not he, had been the one at fault?

'There was nothing wrong with you, Kate, was there?' Abigail probed. 'The fault lay with Jeremy.' Kate's silence was answer enough. 'I understand it was a blackout that caused his accident. Did you know he was a diabetic?'

Kate shook her head, her eyes fluttering away.

'You never suspected?'

'Never.'

As Abigail slipped on her sandals, Kate switched the conversation away from Jeremy, asking diffidently, 'Tell me about your...second husband.'

'Bevan?' The girl's lip curled. 'I thought he was everything I wanted in a man. Powerful, rich, socially impeccable...a man who would give me the world. What a mistake! He's a monster, a heartless, insufferable tyrant. I walked out and came home to lick my wounds...' Her amber eyes suddenly sparked to life. 'And just look who I've been lucky enough to find here! Nick Ramsay has come back home. And, like...wow!'

Kate's eyes flicked to the girl's face. '*Wow*?' she echoed, unable to understand how Abigail, after once being so close to Jeremy, could want to set her cap at Nick—could want anything to do with him. She must know what Nick had done to Jeremy over the years.

Abigail gave a low, rich laugh and tossed her head, causing her red curls to bounce. 'He's quite a hunk, isn't he? I wonder why I never really noticed before? I guess because our paths rarely crossed as we were growing up, or I was too busy chasing after Jeremy. But now...' She heaved a sigh, and, catching Kate's look, said with a pout, 'Oh, dear, you disapprove. Look, I know you must see Nick through Jeremy's jaundiced eyes, Kate, and we all know what Jeremy thought of Nick. But your husband's gone now, darling, and Ramsay Downs should by rights go to Nick. As Sophie Ramsay's son and Logan Ramsay's adopted son...their sole surviving son...Nick does have a genuine claim, you know. And he's always loved the place with a passion...'

'Is that so?' Kate said tautly. She was tempted to bring up Nick's past misdemeanours, but this was hardly the time. Besides, Abigail must be aware of them already. She was simply closing her mind to them, pushing them into the past, as if they no longer existed, or mattered. Abigail, she concluded, was an opportunist. She was the type who'd go after whichever man could offer her the most.

The girl arched a finely tapered eyebrow. 'It can't be the same here, though, now that Jeremy's gone, surely? You're a city girl, and you're all alone now. Why would you want to stay on here?'

Kate inhaled deeply. 'I look on this place as my home,' she said simply, and swinging away, added curtly, 'I think we should go in.'

'Don't be like Jeremy, Kate!' Abigail hurried to catch up with her. 'Don't carry on the hate that ate into him for the whole of his life.'

Kate paused, her heart giving an uneasy dip. Was that what she was doing? Denying Nick his rights because of *hate*? No! She quickly dismissed the notion. The hate, the vindictiveness, had all been on Nick's side. By what he had done in the past, Nick Ramsay had lost any rights he might otherwise have had.

'I'd already made up my mind to stay on here,' she said quietly, 'before Nick turned up. I didn't even know he was back in Australia.'

'Well, Jeremy would be proud of you, Kate,' Abigail said with a faint sneer. 'He was always obsessed with keeping Ramsay Downs out of Nick's hands... and thanks to his dutiful little widow, childless though she might be, it looks as if he's going to achieve his wish!'

Kate felt a shiver of unease ripple down her spine. Expressed in those terms, it sounded quite... shocking. As if she was being deliberately vindictive. Which was so wrong! And yet she couldn't deny there was some truth in what the girl said. Jeremy *had* been obsessed with keeping Ramsay Downs out of Nick's clutches. But hate? Hate, surely, was too strong a word. Nobody could blame Jeremy for not *liking* Nick, for wanting to protect Ramsay Downs from him, after the horrendous things Nick had tried to do to him over the years. Abigail was blowing it all out of proportion, simply because it suited her. Because she was after Nick!

'After you,' she said tightly, pulling open the side door and waving Abigail through. 'I must go in and see Minya about our dinner. Let's meet out on the veranda in...say, half an hour?' By then, she hoped, Danny and James would have come in, and Nick too. And there was safety in numbers. She would make sure, over dinner, that they stuck to station matters.

CHAPTER FIVE

ABIGAIL was an immediate hit with the two young jack-aroos, James and Danny—and with Nick too, Kate suspected, judging by the way he was sitting back, lapping up all the attention she was paying him. *She's going all out to win him over*, she thought, half amused, half irritated, as the girl fluttered her long eyelashes and flashed her dazzling smile, throwing back her head with laughter whenever Nick uttered a witticism or cracked a joke.

'Oh, Nick, it's so *good* to have you back!' she trilled more than once. 'You look just great!' She herself was looking stunning in peacock-green silk, her golden arms bare, her lovely face impeccably made up, and her auburn curls dancing with golden lights under the soft glow of the overhead lamp.

Kate wished she had worn something more alluring than a white cotton-knit top and wrap-around skirt, but, on the other hand, not being the centre of attention allowed her to sit back and listen, and quietly observe. And above all, to think. And she had plenty to think about! Like what Nick Ramsay really thought of his close neighbour and ex-sister-in-law, and what he might be hatching *now* in that fertile mind of his! With a fair idea already of Abigail's likely response to anything he had in mind, she felt her misgivings growing by the second.

Mercifully, no mention was made of Jeremy, or of the past. Chatter about the day's work and the muster planned for the next day, interspersed with jokes and the odd outback yarn, ricocheted non-stop across the table, and before Kate knew it the meal was over and Nick was rising from the table.

'Time I did some work on our new computer,' he said, explaining to Abigail, 'I had it flown out here to make the bookwork easier, and I promised Kate I'd set it up for her.'

'Oh, can't I help?' Abigail sprang to her feet. 'I'm a whizz with a computer, and two heads are better than one.' Her glance flicked to Kate, and back to Nick. 'In fact, if you want a hand any evening at all, just give me a call and I'll ask Dad to fly me over. You'd put me up for the night, wouldn't you, Kate? I've already started doing our bookwork at home, to give Mother a break, so I know what I'm doing.'

Kate opened her mouth to say thanks but no, thanks, they could manage, when Nick spoke up first. 'I guess another pair of hands wouldn't go amiss,' he said easily. 'It's always the setting up part that takes the most time.'

'But surely only one person at a time can use the computer,' Kate heard herself protesting, 'and if you need a helping hand, Nick,' she added firmly, 'I'd rather it was me.' She knew she must sound petty and ungrateful, and possibly a trifle piqued as well, but if she let Nick make all the decisions, she might as well give up and leave now. Or—she took a deep breath—was it simply that she didn't want Abigail working closely with Nick in her own office, undermining her, making a play for Nick, showing her what a great team they made, hoping to make her feel unwanted, unneeded?

She tossed her head, shaking her silky hair away from her face. It certainly wasn't that she cared about Nick and Abigail being together—why should she care? They were two of a kind, both out for what they could get. What bothered her was the thought of them putting their heads together and scheming, right here under her nose, to ease her out!

'Thanks all the same, Abigail,' she added, softening her refusal with a smile. 'Kind of you to offer. Maybe some other time.' When Nick Ramsay, she added silently, is out of my hair, and out of my life.

Abigail's amber eyes hardened in a way that made Kate's resolve waver. She didn't want to make an enemy of Abigail. And she certainly didn't want the girl getting the idea that she had any designs on Nick—heaven forbid! She said hastily, her smile still resolutely in place, 'Look, I'm sure Nick can manage by himself for to-night. You're my guest, Abigail, and I don't intend to neglect a guest. Let's take a stroll outside, shall we, with Danny and James? A breather before we go to bed. It'll be an early start in the morning.'

'You're going on the muster with the men?' A faint frown creased the girl's smooth ivory brow.

'Me?' Kate shook her head. 'No, I have some visitors coming. But I'll be up early to see them all off.'

The girl's auburn head swivelled round. 'Nick, are *you* going on this muster?'

Nick paused as he stepped away from the table. 'Yes, but I won't be leaving with the men. I'll be flying out.'

'Oh, can I come with you? I can help you spot the cattle.'

Kate caught her breath, aware of a sudden tightness in her chest. Abigail seemed determined to get Nick to herself! She imagined the two of them cosily confined in the tiny Cessna all day, getting even friendlier, hatching plans for the future, plans to get rid of *her* ... and she found she was grinding her teeth.

But this time it was Nick who said no. 'Sorry, Abby, but I need all my concentration when I'm doing a muster.' His lips eased into an apologetic smile. 'You'd be too much of a distraction!' His eyes told her precisely what a distraction she would be. 'Besides, it's far too dangerous...there are always some pretty hairy manoeuvres, and I need to throw the plane around. You need a strong stomach and nerves of steel.'

'Oh well, maybe you're right.' Abigail gave in with a charming pout. 'But I'll come and see you off. What time?' she asked brightly.

'We plan to leave around dawn. The men have to get their horses ready first and load them on to the trucks, ready to drive them out to where the cattle are.' His lip quirked. 'You'd be better off getting your beauty sleep.'

'Oh? You think I need it?' She shot him a provocative look.

Nick reached out his arm, the tips of his fingers tweaking her creamy cheek. 'What do you think?' he murmured, and with a quick smile and an airy, 'Goodnight, all,' he swung away from her.

Kate smiled at him through clenched teeth as his eyes swerved round to meet hers fleetingly as he strode past her. Purr, purr, her eyes told him. Abigail certainly has you eating out of her hand. Some men are so...gullible!

She could have sworn she saw a flash of humour in his eyes just before he vanished through the open doorway, as if he'd caught the look, and, far from feeling shamed, was amused by it. He'd better not think I'm jealous, Kate fumed inwardly, clenching her hands into fists. Even if I were...damn it, if he's hoping jealousy will drive me away, he has another think coming!

Abigail's welcome to him, she thought savagely. When he finally gives up and goes away, she can go with him, for all I care. Or they can both go and bury themselves at Doon-gara...assuming Nick would be content to live on a sheep station, and to share Doon-gara with Abigail's brother when he comes home from the Top End. *Would* he?

That's his problem... Kate dismissed the question with a sour glance in the direction he had disappeared. Then, realising that James and Danny were already eagerly ushering Abigail out of the room, she took a deep breath and hastened after them.

'What a glorious night!' Abigail enthused as they crossed the moon-drenched yard. There were no clouds, and the air, cooling rapidly after the day's heat, was crystal-clear. A beautiful balmy night, faintly scented with the fragrance of roses. As James lit a cigarette, Abigail begged, 'May I have one? Normally I don't smoke, but every now and then I weaken...' Her lovely brow puckered in a way that seemed to delight the two young men.

'Sure.' As James thrust out his packet of cigarettes, Danny, quick as a flash, produced a box of matches and lit up for her.

Abigail drew in deeply, at the same time extending a slender hand to take the matchbox from him. 'Unusual pack,' she commented, holding it up and peering closely at the writing on the neat crimson pack. '"The Diplomat, Stockholm"... Well! You've just come back from Sweden, Danny?'

Danny hesitated for a second, then confessed, 'Not me, worse luck—my parents. They've always travelled a lot. They've been bringing me back sample matchboxes for years. I have quite a collection now, from all over the world.'

'Oh well, maybe you'll go yourself some day,' said Abigail, and promptly lost interest in Danny and his matchbox. 'Where are we going?' she asked Kate. She sounded bored now, as if she no longer had a reason to sparkle, now that Nick was no longer present. It was as if she'd decided the two jackaroos were mere adolescents, not worth the effort.

'I thought you might like to take a last look at the polo ponies,' Kate told her, turning towards the stables. As the others followed, a huge bone-white moon, suspended in a sky so transparent that mountains and vast plains were visible on its surface, shed a ghostly pool of light across their path.

'What do you mean—a last look?' Abigail caught her arm. 'You can't mean—you're getting rid of them?'

Kate gulped, and nodded. Reluctantly, she had given Nick the go-ahead to find a buyer, and an agent was due the next day to transport the ponies down to Sydney.

'They're of no use to me,' she said steadily, 'and the money they'll bring in will give me a chance to do...other things.'

'Oh, Kate ... without Jeremy's polo ponies, what will you have left—of Jeremy?' Abigail asked bluntly. 'I truly can't imagine why you'd want to stay on here, without Jeremy, without even his beloved polo ponies to keep his memory alive. It's as if you're discarding the memories of your life together.'

Kate swung her face away as she unlatched the stable door. Was that what she was doing? Discarding the memories of their life together? 'That's not the way I see it,' she said, rallying. 'It's purely economic—the practical thing to do. It won't affect my memories of Jeremy. We had more than a love of horses in common.' Just what *had* they had in common? an insidious voice niggled, deep down inside her. She was startled by the question, and berated herself severely for allowing such an idiotic question to surface in the first place. 'We both loved Ramsay Downs,' she said aloud, a trifle defiantly. 'We both wanted to see it flourish. I'm not going to give up on that, just because ... because ...'

'Oh, Kate, you can't even say it, can you?' Abigail seized on the hesitation. 'Jeremy's dead, Kate. He's *gone* ... and soon even his polo ponies will be gone. And you should go too. Oh, don't take this personally, my dear, but honestly, it's not healthy, an attractive young girl like you, struggling on out here all alone, living in the past, living on memories——'

'I'm not living in the past,' Kate denied swiftly. 'I'm looking to the *future*. Why do you think I'm selling these ponies?' She was becoming exasperated with Abigail. Was the girl genuinely thinking of her? Or was she thinking only of herself, trying to clear the way for herself ... and Nick. And why did the thought of the two of them taking over Ramsay Downs *together* cause another disturbing little niggle inside her? Was it because of Nick's past, because Jeremy, with good reason, had always been so vehemently against Nick ever getting his hands on Ramsay Downs? Or was it ...?

Kate wriggled her shoulders in an attempt to shake off a vague, growing disquiet. It couldn't be anything more than that, anything more ... personal. She'd be all kinds of a fool, knowing the truth about Nick's past, to start softening towards him in any way.

She sighed as she reached up to stroke the velvety nose of Jeremy's favourite, Glory. OK, OK, she acknowledged, determined to be brutally frank with herself, Nick *is* awfully attractive. He's all male, and he makes a girl feel weak at the knees at times, with just a look or a touch. But you'd be crazy, Kate Ramsay, to allow a purely animal reaction to fool you, to influence you in any way. Just keep remembering all the despicable things Nick did to Jeremy over the years, the times he tried to destroy his brother, to drive a wedge between Jeremy and his father, hoping, scheming, that Ramsay Downs would one day go to him, not Jeremy. Just keep those thoughts firmly in your mind, my girl, and you'll be in no danger of weakening. That's precisely what Nick Ramsay is relying on... that you'll come to look on him in a different, gentler light, that you'll end up convinced that Ramsay Downs will flourish in his hands, until in the end you'll give in and hand everything over to him.

Everything... with Abigail, by the look of it, thrown in!

And she, Kate...what would she have? Nothing worth that much! She snapped her fingers—and the sound snapped her back to earth. She glanced round, her startled green eyes gradually focusing, meeting Abigail's speculative stare.

The birds were already up and about, making a tremendous din, when Kate emerged from the house at dawn, pulling her sweater more tightly round her shoulders. It would undoubtedly be hot later in the day, but right now, with the sun no more than a vivid orange streak on the horizon, the air was still crisp and icy.

There was a lot of shouting as the men saddled their mounts for the long truck-drive ahead. Saddle leather creaked, and horses' hoofs rang out sharply on the rocky ground, their breath, like misty plumes, streaming from their mouths into the icy air.

She smiled as she saw Danny tug the brim of his hat lower and turn up the collar of his leather jacket against the cold. He was trying to look nonchalant, but he couldn't hide the excitement in his eyes at the prospect of the muster ahead.

Suddenly she heard a shout that was louder than the rest, and her stomach churned as her ears picked up the words.

'Glory's gone! Who in hell's name left the stable door open?'

Nick's towering figure materialised from the gloom, and as Kate hurried towards him, she yelled to a passing stockman, 'Saddle up my horse—pronto!' In the same breath she gasped at Nick, 'Any idea how long since she got out? She can't have gone far!'

'Don't count on it.' Nick's tone was grim. 'There were brumbies around here last night. If she's joined up with them . . .' He swore.

'You *saw* the brumbies?'

'No, but I heard them. While I was out taking a late stroll . . .' He turned to shout at the men gathering round on their mounts. 'You lot go along the river . . . You others skirt the home paddock. I'll go east. Danny, Joe, Smithy, you come with me!' He grabbed the nearest spare horse—*her* horse, Kate noticed in stunned disbelief— and vaulted into the saddle.

'Get off my horse!' she shouted.

'No time to waste . . . I'm going after those brumbies!' He jerked the palomino round, gave a high-pitched yell, and thundered off, with Danny and the two stockmen at his heels.

Kate stamped her feet in fury. 'You've gone too far this time, Nick Ramsay! You bring back my horse!'

She was talking to herself. 'James!' she bellowed, spying the young jackaroo's stocky figure vaulting into the saddle of the big grey. 'I'll take Silver—you find another mount!'

James knew better than to argue with the boss, especially in her present mood. 'Sure, Kate, sure,' he said, sliding from the saddle. 'But you're not going after the brumbies, are you? That's no job for a——' His voice trailed off, a look from Kate quelling further argument.

'Glory knows me better than anyone,' she gasped as she seized the reins from him. 'If she's gone off with the brumbies, I just might...' She didn't waste time explaining, but threw herself into the saddle and urged the big grey into a gallop, following the clouds of dust which showed the direction Nick and the others had taken.

The blazing tip of the dawning sun was sending long fingers of gold through the tea-tree scrub as she thundered after them, hunched in the saddle to avoid the thin branches whipping at her face, plucking at her clothes. She was on their heels as they broke out of the scrub, sending several wallabies bolting before them, their small grey bodies vanishing like lightning into the thick undergrowth.

Kate's heart gave a leap as she heard a wild cry ahead, above the frantic pounding of hoofbeats, '*Brumbies*!' She saw Nick streak away from the others, half standing in his stirrups, leaning well forward, like a jockey with his eye fixed on the winning post. She gave a shriek of her own to spur Silver on, and flew after him, narrowing her eyes in determination as she inched past first Joe, then Smithy, then finally past Danny, catching a glimpse of the young jackaroo's face, his eyes bright with excitement, his lips peeled back in a grin as he strove to keep up with her.

Kate caught sight of the runaway chestnut at the same moment Nick did, the pony's golden mane streaming behind as she kept pace with the thundering mob. She saw Nick wheel around to head the pony off, riding with heart-stopping speed and a skill to match, and crouching low, she thundered in to help.

She had a glimpse of the sudden horror in Nick's eyes as he glanced round and saw her, heard his bark of warning, 'Careful, Kate, stay back!'

She didn't falter, shouting, 'Come on, Glory, come on, good girl!' as she flew after Nick, hoping the familiar sound of her voice, assuming it carried over the thunder of the hoofbeats, would have a reassuring effect on the pony.

Glory's ears pricked in response to her voice as Nick, cracking his stockwhip, streaked round and steered the frightened animal away from the mob, with Kate closing in on the chestnut's opposite flank, seconds before the three stockmen pounded in from behind.

As the rest of the herd plunged wildly away, Kate reined in the big grey and swung round to face Nick, torn between admiration for what he'd done for her and anger at the way he'd gone about it, whisking her horse away in the face of her protests. Admiration won, and she smiled at him, her eyes softening in a silent thank-you. As their eyes met she saw something flare in the black depths, a kind of anguished relief, and a great leaping emotion hit her deep inside. Then the stockmen were crowding around them and they broke eye contact and turned their attention to the snorting, quivering pony.

As they led the exhausted chestnut back to the homestead, Nick sent Smithy on ahead to signal to the others by means of a single gunshot, their prearranged signal, that the mare had been found, and that the muster could go ahead.

'We could have lost Glory,' Kate conceded, knowing it was thanks to Nick's prompt action that they hadn't.

'Thanks,' she said. But now that the initial elation was subsiding, she couldn't prevent a faint coolness creeping into her voice. Nobody, not even Nick Ramsay, overseer or not, was entitled to grab the boss's mare from under her very nose and ignore her express command to bring her back at once.

Nick turned to her with a sheepish grin. 'Sorry about your horse, Kate, but any delay could have been fatal. Thanks for coming out to help. But you took a hell of a risk. I could hardly believe it when I saw you right there behind me...you must have ridden like the wind!'

There was a glint of something else in his eyes now— surprise, Kate suspected, and maybe even admiration— that caused her to run her tongue along her lips, feeling vaguely unnerved. Hadn't he expected her to come after him? Hadn't he known she could outride most of the men here, even the Aboriginal stockmen?

'Thanks for finding her so quickly,' she said, her annoyance subsiding. At least he hadn't said that a brumby chase was no place for a woman. 'But how on earth do you think Glory got out in the first place? I was in the stables last night, and I made sure the door was securely fastened.' She paused as a memory stirred. 'You said you went out for a stroll later. Did you happen to check the door?'

'No, I didn't, more's the pity. I didn't go near the stables,' Nick answered, but something in his tone, and the way he turned his head away, as if avoiding her eye, brought a swift frown to her brow. Had he remembered seeing something? Or didn't he want to be interrogated, for some reason?

'Why did you go out last night, anyway?' she pressed on, determined to get to the bottom of it. Or at least to have a good try.

He didn't answer for a second. Then, 'Abigail couldn't sleep,' he said smoothly, still not facing her directly. 'We . . . took a stroll together. That was when we heard the brumbies . . . some distance away, admittedly. Still, I guess I ought to have checked the stables, made sure they were secure.'

Was that why he was avoiding her eye? Because he felt he had fallen down on his job, and he felt guilty about it? Or was it because of his secret tryst with Abigail?

'No doubt you had other things on your mind,' she said rather waspishly. Why should it bother her so much, the thought of Nick taking a midnight stroll with Abigail? Not that it was that so much . . . it was the thought of what might have happened *afterwards*. With that thought came another, and with that, a dreadful suspicion.

What if the two of them had planned this whole thing; had planned Glory's escape, deliberately taking the risk of the pony running off with the brumbies . . . just so that Nick could go racing off to the rescue, and come back, triumphant, with the pony in tow! And why? So that she, Kate, would be so grateful to Nick, so much in his debt, that she would come one step closer to handing the station over to him, knowing that when she did the place would be in good safe hands!

It seemed far-fetched, but knowing what Nick Ramsay was capable of, perhaps not so far-fetched. He could, of course, have planned it entirely on his own, without Abigail knowing anything about it. But the two of them *had* been together last night . . . for goodness knew how long. Kate felt a sick anger wash through her. Had they teamed up already, the two of them, to try to force her out?

What else had they teamed up to do? she wondered, lapsing into a brooding silence. To make a cosy little twosome in the future? A *permanent* twosome? *Already*? Her slender hands tightened on the leather reins. Why was it that this second thought was even harder to accept than the first?

She maintained her silence for the rest of the ride back, only vaguely noticing that the sun was well up in the sky by now, its warmth already dissolving the early morning mist and gradually taking the chill from the air. When they rode into the stables they found the place virtually deserted, the stockmen having already loaded their mounts on to the trucks and driven off. Only Tom, the rouseabout, was there to meet them, and...

Kate's heart dipped as Abigail came flying across the yard, a vision of loveliness in her bronze trousers and cream shirt, her face already carefully made up, her red curls caught back in a jaunty black bow. Kate was suddenly conscious of how she must look herself, with no make-up, her hair tangled from her ride through the bush, her hands scratched, and no doubt her face as well, and her shirt all awry, plucked out of her jeans during the chase.

'Nick—oh, Nick, you're a *marvel*!' Abigail reached up to catch Nick's hand in both of hers. 'You've saved Glory! Everyone here went crazy when they heard—they said they wouldn't know what on earth the place would do without you!'

Nick said nothing, but he looked down into her face for rather longer than was necessary, Kate thought sourly, her suspicions rekindling. She turned away, not wanting to witness the way his dark eyes must be softening as they drank in the sight of the girl—and then wishing seconds later, when it was too late, that she *had* watched, to see if his eyes revealed anything else—mutual triumph, perhaps, or elation, at the successful outcome of their midnight plotting.

'You'd better get back home before the heat of the day hits,' she heard him advising Abigail. So concerned for her welfare! Kate thought, her green eyes throwing mental daggers at him. *If you want to pursue Abigail, Nick Ramsay, you go ahead—but do your courting on her property, not mine!*

Nick's head swivelled round unexpectedly, and his gaze caught hers, and narrowed in what seemed to her to be faint consternation, almost as if he had read her thoughts. The look was quickly gone, and he said easily, 'I'll be off, then. I'll be back at lunchtime, Kate, to refuel, but I won't come back to the house—Minya's prepared me a cut lunch. Don't wait dinner for me . . . I may be late back.' He swung on his heel, and, raising his voice, commanded, 'Tom, drive me out to the plane, will you?'

'Bye-bye, Nick!' Abigail called after him as he strode off. 'Are they bringing the cattle back here?' she asked without even glancing at Kate, her eyes on Nick's retreating figure, a secret smile on her lips.

'No,' said Kate. 'They'll be loading them on to a cattle truck up there. Someone's coming down from Winton to pick them up.' But she was talking to herself. Abigail was already swinging away in the direction of the Big House, calling cheerfully over her shoulder, 'I'll just grab my things from the house and be off.'

With Nick gone, Abigail wasted no time leaving, neither she nor Kate making any plans to meet again. But both knew that they would . . . later, Kate profoundly hoped, rather than sooner.

CHAPTER SIX

KATE drove out herself to meet Nick's plane when she heard him buzzing the homestead around dusk. She was anxious to hear how the muster was going, and to tell Nick about her own day, mostly taken up with the agent who had come for the polo ponies. She was surprised at how long the day had seemed without him.

She drew in a sharp breath at the thought, horrified at the implication that she might actually have missed him. It was not Nick, the *man*, she had missed, she quickly assured herself. It was just that she was anxious to hear about the day's muster. The day she started missing Nick Ramsay, the *man* ... Heavens, she'd have to be crazy to want to get embroiled with a man she had so little regard for ... a man who had gone through life filled with hate and envy and thoughts of revenge, a man who was only here because of *greed*, not out of any real sentiment for Ramsay Downs!

Anyway, as if he would ever want to get embroiled with *her*, his despised brother's widow. She knew far too much about him. In any dispute, she would always have too much to throw back in his face.

That alone should make her safe.

When Nick stepped down from the plane there was no smiling welcome, no danger of getting emotionally embroiled in any way. His face was grim.

'Get back in the car,' he ordered curtly. 'I'll drive.'

Bewildered, wondering what on earth had put him in such a foul mood, Kate meekly obeyed. As the engine roared to angry life and the vehicle slewed away from the airstrip, churning up dust, he explained.

'Something's wrong out in the home paddock. A couple of the calves are in some kind of trouble—saw them as I flew in. And soon it'll be too dark to see.'

Kate turned a shocked face to his. 'I haven't been out there today. I was too busy with the——'

'Never mind. Open that gate, will you?' As the jeep lurched to a halt, she jumped out, only just managing to swing the gate shut again and jump back in as the vehicle shot forward again.

She gave a cry, her heart twisting in sympathy as they pulled up near the water trough in the gathering gloom. Two young calves, their small bodies distended, were having violent spasms and difficulty breathing. Their mother was hovering nearby, while the rest of the herd, several cows with their calves, were watching from a distance, seemingly unaffected by whatever was causing the calves' distress.

Nick swore as he leapt out to examine the ailing animals. 'Looks like strychnine poisoning!' he muttered in disgust. 'We'll need to make them vomit. Got your radio handy, Kate? Get Tom to rush out some water and salt— plenty of it! If we can make them vomit we might be able to save them!'

Kate grabbed the radio, her heart sinking. '*Strychnine poisoning*', Nick had said. That could only mean . . . But she couldn't think about that now. She babbled out the message, then turned to Nick and moaned, 'But *how*? How could they have been poisoned?'

Without answering, he moved across to the water trough. Kate's hand flew to her lips.

'You think——'

Scooping up some water in his cupped hands, Nick bent down to drink.

'Be careful, Nick!'

'Ugh!' He spat it out. 'Bitter!'

Kate swallowed hard. 'You mean——'

'Looks as if someone's poured strychnine into our water trough. Maybe not enough to kill a cow, but——' he straightened, his eyes gleaming black pools in the eerie half-light '—enough to threaten the life of a young calf. Keep the rest of the herd away, will you? We'll move them later. Just as well I saw those two calves when I did.'

'Oh, Nick, I'm so grateful! Thank you!' She looked up at him, her eyes misty with relief. But for Nick, she could have lost every calf in the paddock! Realising she was grasping his arm, she flushed, and would have let her hand drop away, only before she could he brought his other hand up and closed it over hers.

'It'll be all right, Kate.' Though his voice was still grim, his hand was warm and soothing on hers. His head flicked round as he heard the station ute. 'Here's Tom now.'

'Thank God!' Kate breathed.

When they both came back to the Big House, chilled and exhausted later in the evening after tending the stricken calves and moving the rest of the herd, Minya insisted on warming them both up with some hot soup and steak and kidney pie, serving the meal on trays in the den. As they ate, Nick brought Kate up to date on the day's muster, and listened sympathetically as she related, in a pensive tone, how she had helped the buyer from Sydney load the polo ponies into his horse van to be carted away. Over their coffee, the conversation, inevitably, swung back to the drama in the home paddock.

'But who on earth would pour *strychnine* into our water trough and poison our calves?' Baffled, Kate shook her head. 'It—it had to be deliberate. I—I simply can't believe it!'

Nick didn't answer for a moment, glowering into his coffee as if deep in thought. When he looked up, any expression in the brooding black eyes was shadowed by his thick lowered brows. 'Someone who holds a grudge against you, Kate?' he suggested quietly. 'Perhaps your former overseer? Or someone else you've sent packing?'

Kate's hand flew to her lips. Leif Clancy! Could it be possible? Could he resent her, despise her, that much, for what she had done to him?

'No, it can't be Leif.' She shook her head. 'Smithy heard that he and Annie had found work up Longreach way.'

Nick stroked his chin. 'That's not so far away. Depends how determined he was to get back at you. Not that you'd ever be able to prove it,' he muttered with a shrug. 'We'll just have to keep a closer watch on things. Try not to worry, Kate . . . it could have been a lot worse. We could have lost those two calves—and maybe a whole lot more, if I hadn't noticed something was wrong from the air.' He started to talk about something else—rather too quickly, Kate thought, her deep-down mistrust of the man flaring suddenly to renewed life.

As he talked, she eyed him speculatively over the rim of her coffee cup. He had come to her rescue again, and saved her calves, just as he had saved Glory earlier in the day. And he'd made sure that she knew it too—and was grateful to him. But what if *he* . . .?

Her heart went cold. No, it was too far-fetched, too... monstrous.

But was it? She stirred restlessly in her chair, fingering her coffee-cup in distress. Nick Ramsay must resent her every bit as much as Leif Clancy did—perhaps even more. He had never hidden the fact that he wanted her gone. Furthermore, Nick was right here on the spot, whereas Leif Clancy was reportedly miles away. And Nick Ramsay had never been averse, in the past, to a little skulduggery to get what he wanted. Maybe, in this case, his intention had been simply to frighten her, hoping to *scare* her away...

But to deliberately jeopardise the lives of helpless young calves... No, it was impossible. Nick couldn't have done it. He had been away mustering all day...

Kate drew in a ragged breath. No, not quite *all* day. Nick had flown back to the property at lunchtime to refuel, and she had been busy at the time with the polo ponies. He would have had the time... the opportunity... and there would have been no danger of witnesses, with the men away at the muster.

No... *No*! Something else deep inside her, something more powerful even than her mistrust, rebelled at the thought, rejected it. Nick would never do that to her... harm her stock, endanger the lives of defenceless calves, no matter how much he might want to drive her out. She was overtired, overwrought, she was becoming hysterical. It couldn't be true... it was too horrendous to contemplate.

'I—I'd better get to bed,' she said in a muffled voice, running a distracted hand through her hair. 'I—I'm just so tired.' Tired? She was physically and emotionally exhausted! After a good long sleep perhaps she would see things differently, see how ridiculous she was being.

Nick could have left the calves to die, could have let the whole herd suffer, but he hadn't. He was trying to help her, not deliberately plotting setbacks, disasters, to discourage and scare her away, or to demonstrate how he could run this place better than she could, regardless of any animals he might hurt in the process. That would make him a monster—even more of a monster than Jeremy had painted him. And he wasn't.

He couldn't be!

As she scraped back her chair and stood up, she glanced across at him, and for a dizzying second his face blurred, and she saw Jeremy's face instead, staring back at her with bitter reproach and pity, as if to say, 'Oh, Kate, who are you kidding? Two incidents in one day! First Glory, and now a poisoning. Someone has to be behind it all. Someone who resents you being here, who wants to break your spirit. Who else can it be but my demonic younger brother? He has the most to gain...'

She turned sharply, blinking the image away. 'Excuse me,' she croaked, 'I must...' Her voice failed her, and she let her hands flutter in the air. Was this only the beginning? Would there be more incidents, more near-tragedies? Perhaps she could even be in some personal danger herself!

Her heart squeezed in an agony of doubt and despair.

As she stumbled blindly away she felt a warm hand close over her arm, and she swung round, her breath catching in her throat, her eyes huge and liquid in her pale face.

'What——?'

'Don't be frightened, Kate.' Nick was standing over her, his hand steadying her, his powerful frame between her and the lamp behind, blotting out the light. 'I won't let anything happen to you.'

She stared up at him, her eyes pained, yearning, wishing his face weren't in shadow, wishing she could read what was in those fathomless black eyes. If only she could believe him!

'Come here, Kate.'

She gulped, her bones suddenly liquefying as he pulled her into his arms, not capable of resisting as he brought one hand up and threaded his fingers through her hair, cradling her head against his shoulder. 'You've had a nasty shock, Kate...but it will be all right, I promise you.'

How warm and safe, how *right* it felt in his arms, with the heat of his body warming her, his hard-muscled chest pressed hard against her cheek! She was aware of the tension flowing out of her, of his body's warmth and strength flowing into hers, spreading along her veins, giving her comfort and strength.

She could have stayed there forever, blissfully snug and safe, happily believing every word he said. But— she stirred uneasily in his arms—wasn't that precisely what he wanted? Her trust, her belief in him, her confidence in his capabilities? Next, if she didn't take care, she would be urging him, 'Take Ramsay Downs, Nick, take it all. I know I'll be leaving it in good hands.' And that would be a disaster! It would be betraying Jeremy's trust in her...to say nothing of betraying her own deep love for Ramsay Downs, her own needs.

Her own needs? And precisely what were her own needs? Why did she feel so confused, so uncertain, so *torn*?

She choked back a sob, and, afraid that she was going to weaken further and burst into helpless tears, she summoned the last vestiges of her flagging will-power and tore herself from his arms. Without daring to glance up at him, she spun round and fled.

She woke early after a surprisingly sound night's sleep, with a clearer head and a more balanced perspective on the events of the previous evening. *She* was the monstrous one, to even think for a second that Nick would have deliberately staged such a shocking near-tragedy. Nick loved animals, he cared deeply for their welfare—she had seen evidence of it, again and again. He would never risk hurting the stock, especially not vulnerable young calves ... not deliberately, in cold blood.

It had to be someone else, perhaps a stranger passing through, jealous of her good fortune—a simple act of spite. Or perhaps Leif Clancy actually *had* come back, resentful enough to go to any lengths to hit back at her. They would probably never know for sure. And as Nick had said, even if they did suspect someone, how could they ever prove it? They would just have to be more careful in the future.

To make amends for her unforgivable suspicions, and to show Nick that she had fully recovered from the shock of the night before and wasn't going to let what had happened overcome her, she went out of her way to be bright and cheerful when they met in the yard, offering to drive him out to the airstrip when he was ready to fly out to continue the muster, and waving him off with a warm smile.

As the plane taxied away, she hugged to herself the memory of his parting words, the way he had paused before climbing up into the plane, peering into her face for a long moment with a softer than usual look in his eyes, a new tenderness which, although she wasn't sure what it meant, had a distinctly weakening effect on her.

'You look after yourself, Kate. Understand?'

'Understood.' She stayed where she was for some time, watching until the plane soared upward and became a tiny speck in the misty blue sky, her hand raised to shade her eyes against the brightness of the early morning sun. Her heart felt inexplicably lighter. He had seemed genuinely concerned for her welfare. Surely he wouldn't feel like that if he had—if he——?

She sighed, and turned to back to the jeep, a faint mistiness in her eyes. If only things had been different. If only Nick had been someone else, a stranger to her, a stranger to Jeremy. If only...

But to think that way was madness.

When Nick flew back at lunchtime to refuel Kate was there at the airstrip to meet him, handing him a cut lunch that she had prepared herself. He seemed to appreciate it, his gaze resting on her face with a burning intentness that brought a rush of colour to her cheeks.

'Everything all right?' he asked, and she swallowed, and nodded, wondering at the concern in his eyes. Was he afraid there might have been further disasters while he was away?

'Sure. Everything's fine.'

'Good. We should have the muster all wrapped up in a couple of hours, and then the men can start heading back. With those clouds starting to roll in, I reckon we'll be just in time. Looks as if we might have a storm later.'

'You'll be careful, Nick, won't you?' Kate said impulsively, and hastily glanced away as her eyes collided with his, afraid of what her own might be revealing.

'I will. You take care too. I'll be back as soon as I can.' His voice was a deep rumble, warm and reassuring. She had the silliest feeling that, as long as Nick had anything to do with it, she would indeed be perfectly safe, and so would he. Which was so foolish, dangerously foolish, she thought, sighing. Relying on Nick Ramsay, of all people.

Dark clouds were rolling in, and there was thunder in the air when Nick flew in around dusk. Kate had been anxiously eyeing them for some time before she heard the reassuring buzz of the Cessna overhead. She was waiting on the airstrip, leaning against the door of the jeep, when he landed, bringing the small plane to a smooth halt only metres away.

'What's wrong?' Nick asked sharply, noting her wince as she turned to climb into the jeep.

'It's nothing...just my neck,' she admitted, giving it a rueful rub. 'It's a bit sore...it's been coming on all day.'

'How did it happen?' he asked, and she heard the same concern in his voice that had been there earlier in the day. It sent a warm quiver through her.

'It must have happened when I was helping Tom unload some timber.'

He frowned. 'You shouldn't be doing that.'

'Look, it's nothing, truly. A hot bath'll fix it.'

Trying not to react to the touch of his hand on her arm, she hauled herself up into the front seat and started up the engine. On the short drive back to the Big House she questioned him about the muster, glad to hear that it had gone well and that the men would be back home by the next morning. When they reached the homestead, she stepped out gingerly, agreeing to meet Nick again in ten minutes for a drink on the veranda. After dinner, she decided, she would make an early escape and take a soaking hot bath. It would give her an excuse not to linger too long in his company. She was becoming far too dangerously vulnerable to Nick Ramsay, and it would be foolish, very foolish, if she let her feelings for him get out of control. Wisest, for her own peace of mind, to keep him at arm's length from now on.

Not that last night's embrace had meant anything— she wasn't that silly. He had only been comforting her, reassuring her, demonstrating once again that *he* was in command and that she could rely on him to sweep in and put things right...showing her, as he loved to do, that he was the best one to look after Ramsay Downs, and, if she would only bow out and leave it all to him, he could get on with it!

She mustn't make the mistake of being fooled by such clever little ploys, by any false sentiment on his side. Regardless of whether or not Nick had planted that poison himself—and she simply couldn't, wouldn't, lay such a monstrous act at Nick's door—no matter what he might have done in the past, he had, deliberately or otherwise, turned the situation to his own advantage, racing to the rescue, taking the credit for preventing further possible tragedies. She must never trust him, no matter how tempted she might be. Everything he did was calculated...for his own benefit. She had learned that from Jeremy, and it was a lesson she must never forget.

She rose from the table just as Minya came in to clear away the plates.

'Don't you want coffee?' asked Minya, glancing from Kate to Nick, her narrowed black eyes showing no expression as they flicked past Kate's face, but visibly crinkling when they came to rest on Nick's. Kate was used to it now—to the way Minya softened in Nick's presence.

'Not for me, thanks, Minya,' she said with a shake of her head, biting back a gasp as the movement caused a stabbing pain in her neck. 'I'm going to take a hot bath,' she said, reaching up to rub her neck. 'Why don't *you* have some coffee with Nick, Minya?' The two didn't often get the chance to be alone together. Was she being foolish to encourage it? The two who had the most reason to want her gone?

'Good idea,' Nick said at once. 'Bring it out to the veranda, would you, Minya? After that I'll go and do some more work on the computer.' He rose as Minya, flashing one of her rare smiles, gathered up their plates and shuffled out. 'Before you go, Kate...'

'Yes?' Kate paused, drawing in a quick breath as he swung towards her.

He moved round behind her. 'Where does it hurt? Here?' His fingers gently stroked the spot where her own fingers had been a second ago.

'Yes, there... all around.' She took in another breath, a deeper one this time, shivering faintly under his touch. He smelt faintly of soap and aftershave, and some special male fragrance of his own.

With the fingers of both hands resting on either side of her neck, he began to rotate his thumbs at her nape, gently kneading her muscles.

She let out a long sigh. 'That feels good!'

'Don't speak... just relax.' He gradually increased the pressure, and she could feel his hot breath on her neck, the radiating warmth of his powerful frame close behind her, even though their bodies weren't actually touching. She closed her eyes, her breathing quickening, trembling at his closeness, at the exquisite sensations quivering through her. She was tempted to lean back, to feel the full length of his body pressed against hers, to experience even more sensation.

It was madness, and she knew it, but she made no effort to resist the feeling, to break away, knowing she couldn't have resisted if she'd tried. Never before had she felt such simmering excitement, such exquisite pleasure, such trembling anticipation. Jeremy had never been one to indulge in tender moments like this; he had been too impatient, always in too much of a hurry. Even in their most intimate moments together he had lacked sensitivity, lacked consideration, never bothering with sensitive foreplay; he had always been too eager to achieve his own satisfaction, too eager to get her pregnant... and when, after months of disappointment, he'd realised that that was never going to happen, he had gradually withdrawn, eventually turning away from her altogether, with no thought for the pain and emptiness she might have been experiencing too.

But this... this was delicious... it was sheer bliss.

She forgot about the pain in her neck, forgot everything but the sensations running riot inside her, every nerve end tinglingly aware of the hypnotic motion of Nick's fingers on her neck and shoulders, each fingertip sending a tingling electric charge into her flesh, turning her whole body into liquid fire.

When he gently spun her round, trailing his fingers lightly across her throat, she still didn't resist, couldn't resist, not even when he brought his lips down on hers. Far from resisting, she went even further and pressed her lips to his in a wave of need, drinking from them, ravenously, as if she were suffering a raging thirst.

She was only dimly aware of the shrill of the telephone in the next room, only dimly aware that it had fallen silent again after only a couple of rings, her hands sliding up of their own accord to curl around Nick's neck, her lips all the while moving under his, feeling his tongue sliding between her teeth, flicking over hers.

'Ma'am...*ma'am*!' An insistent voice intruded, harsh as sandpaper.

Slowly, reluctantly, Kate drew back, away from Nick, her head still spinning from his kiss. From *their* kiss, she amended in dawning dismay. She was every bit as responsible as he was. Dear heaven, she had practically thrown herself at him! What on earth had she been thinking of? What on earth must he be thinking? What must *Minya* be thinking?

'What is it, Minya?' she asked, more sharply than she intended. Only Minya called her 'ma'am', still refusing to call her Kate, like everyone else.

Minya took a step closer, her small black eyes inscrutable, her weathered face stiff. With disapproval, Kate had no doubt. Minya wouldn't relish seeing Jeremy's widow in the arms of her precious Nick, kissing him, leading him on. Minya, like Nick himself, would like to see her gone.

'There's a phone call for you,' Minya rasped. 'It's Abigail Stanton.'

Kate's breath hissed through her teeth. That was all she needed! But at least it gave her the chance to escape.

'Thank you, Minya.' She didn't even glance at Nick as she forced her legs to propel her hastily from the room.

'Hi, Kate.' Abigail's honeyed tone put Kate on full alert. What did her neighbour want this time? 'How's the muster going? Is Nick back yet?'

Kate compressed her lips. No 'How are you? How was your day?' Obviously, all she cared about was Nick!

'The muster's all done. And yes, Nick's here. Do you want to speak to him?'

'In a minute, yes. I'm calling to invite you to a small celebration.'

Kate's brow puckered. 'A celebration?' She pursed her lips. Abigail's divorce, no doubt. Nick *will* be pleased, she thought caustically. Knowing she's free, he'll be able to move right in. Maybe then, she thought, hardening her heart, he'll stop playing around with *me*. Because that's all he's been doing, she told herself harshly. The sympathy over her sore neck, the kisses—they were just to soften her up, to put him in a better light. All he wanted—all he'd ever wanted—was for her to leave, to go back home 'where she belonged'.

She sighed tremulously. Nick had never made any secret of the fact that he wanted her to go. A few kisses, to Nick Ramsay, were simply a means to an end, a way of softening her up. How he must be secretly laughing, being well aware that she, to her shame, had actually encouraged his kisses this time! She stifled a groan.

'Kate, are you still there? Did you hear me? I said, it's an engagement party.'

'An engagement?' Kate spun back to earth. 'Sorry, Abigail. Yes, I heard you.' Her heart constricted. 'Who——?'

'My brother Teddy. He's come home, bringing his brand-new fiancée with him. Love at first sight, he tells me,' Abigail added drily. 'They plan to get married in a couple of months.'

'Oh, that's——'

'Yes, sure, it's just great.' Abigail didn't sound particularly elated. 'Somehow I can't imagine my baby brother married. I thought it would be years before...' She trailed off with a sigh.

'They're going to settle down...at Doon-gara?' Kate asked tentatively.

'Where else?' Abigail said broodingly. 'My parents intend to move to the Gold Coast after the wedding, and leave Doon-gara to them...to us.'

'I see,' Kate said slowly. Was Abigail's nose out of joint because she had been hoping to share Doon-gara with her brother—just the two of them—and now she was faced with having to share it with his wife as well? Two mistresses at Doon-gara! Would Abigail still want to stay on there after her brother was married? Or would she be more determined than ever now to get her claws into Nick, hoping to move into Ramsay Downs one day, with him? Kate felt a stir of jealousy, and frowned, dismissing the sentiment. Jealousy? What rot! It was just the thought of the two of them taking over *her* home.

'As I said, we're having an engagement party for them.' Abigail came back to the point of her call. 'A Sunday lunchtime barbecue. Want to come? I'll be asking Nick too, of course. And why don't you bring Danny and James along too?'

'Oh, sure. That would be...lovely.' Kate tried to sound enthusiastic. 'Just a minute and I'll put Nick on.'

Catching sight of Minya, she asked her to call Nick in. She didn't want to see him just now, if she could help it. As Minya nodded and headed for the door, Kate dropped the phone and fled to her room.

CHAPTER SEVEN

'How's the neck?' Nick asked the next morning, his burning black glance catching hers, bringing two spots of bright colour to her cheeks.

'Much better, thanks.' Flicking a look up at the sky, Kate hastily changed the subject. 'Those clouds didn't come to much—only one sharp shower and a few drops of thundery rain overnight. It's passing over already.'

'The guys will be thankful . . . they aren't likely to get bogged on their way home,' Nick said easily. He sounded amused, as if he had guessed that the weather was simply a ploy to divert him from more personal talk.

She said briskly, 'I'm going out to check on those calves and cows. Care to help me bring them back into the home paddock? I've already scrubbed out the water trough and refilled it with fresh water.' She gulped. What if . . . ?

Nick brushed his fingers over her cheek, and she almost leapt back, stung at the feathery touch, light as it was. 'You're afraid someone might have tampered with it again?' His eyes held a perceptive warmth that made her tremble. 'Let's take a look, shall we? We'll ride out.'

'OK,' she said, turning swiftly away.

To their heartfelt relief they found nothing amiss. But later in the day, when the stockmen's truck arrived back, James and Danny brought further bad news.

'The windmill out at the five-mile . . . some idiot's poured sand and cement into it!'

'Hell's...teeth!' Nick ground out. He turned to Kate, saw blood draining from her cheeks, and in two strides he was standing over her, his hands firmly clasping her shoulders, his lips tight, his jaw granite-hard. 'I'll get to the bottom of this, Kate, don't you worry. It's got to stop!'

Her dazed eyes gradually focused on his, bemused by the fierce flame she saw flickering in the black depths. He seemed so angry, so concerned! Was his anger, his concern genuine? If only she could know for sure! 'What—what are you going to do?' she whispered.

'There must be tracks... tell-tale marks of some kind. If there are, I'll find them. You stay here, Kate. Leave it to me!'

Leave it to him? Kate felt her body sag as he released her. Once again he was sweeping off to the rescue, expecting her to rely on him to put things right. The funny thing was, the ridiculous thing was, he made her actually believe that she could rely on him!

She ran the tip of her tongue over her lips. What kind of fool did that make her? Relying on Nick Ramsay... leaving everything to him. Wasn't that precisely what he'd always wanted?

As Nick strode off, the heels of his boots kicking up red dust, she realised that James was eyeing her oddly. Catching her eye, the lad said in a rallying tone, 'If anyone can find any tracks, Kate, it will be Nick. He's the best bush-tracker I've ever known. He's as good as any Aboriginal tracker. But then he *is*...I mean, it's in his——' He stopped, clamping his teeth on his lip, his chubby face flaming.

'In his blood,' Kate finished, nodding. 'He's not ashamed of it, James.'

'No, of course not.' James looked abashed.

It was dinnertime before Nick came back. Kate was pacing the veranda, toying with a glass of mineral water. 'Did you find anything?' she asked breathlessly.

'Afraid not,' he said grimly. 'There was just enough rain in the night to obliterate any tracks.'

Had there been? Despite herself, Kate felt a flare of doubt, of the old mistrust. There had certainly been some rain, but not much. What if...? She bowed her head over her glass, letting honeyed strands of hair spill across her face. What if Nick had deliberately obliterated his own tracks?

She stifled a groan. Would she never be free of these doubts, this confusion, this sensation of being tossed first in one direction, then another? She had a sudden vivid image of Jeremy's face, his blue eyes approving. He seemed to be saying, 'I know it's not easy, Kate, but you've got to hang in there. He's devilishly clever...he'll try anything to get his hands on your property...you mustn't let him fool you'.

She jumped as if stung when Nick's hand touched hers. 'You're frightened, Kate, aren't you?' he asked, his tone gentle now.

She raised her face slowly to his, realising in dismay that she must have groaned aloud. And that he had read it as fear. Did she have reason to be frightened? she wondered, a cold hand closing over her heart. And if she did, why should he care?

'Kate, I want you to go home, just for a while...'

Her head snapped back. 'This is my home!'

'I mean your old home, Kate, in Sydney. Stay with your family for a while... or friends... until I've sorted this out. There've been too many things, one on top of the other. First Glory, then the poisoned water trough, and now... this. Who's to know what—or *who*—will be targeted next? I want you safe, Kate.'

Her eyes clung to his, searching, shadowed with a painful uncertainty. Staring into the earnest black depths, it was hard not to believe that he meant it. But Jeremy's vision a moment ago had reminded her just how clever, how ruthless Nick Ramsay could be. Did he want her safe, or just... out of the way? Hoping that once she'd had a taste of Sydney, of the comforts and safety of home, of the company of friends and relatives, she wouldn't want to come back!

She tore her eyes away from his. 'I'm not leaving. I intend to help you get to the bottom of all this.' Was she being foolhardy? Putting herself at risk? Would her stubbornness, her refusal, goad him—assuming he actually was responsible for all this—into going even further, to even more dramatic lengths to drive her away? By staying, was she putting herself in very real danger?

'I want you safe,' Nick had said a moment ago. That could be a warning of sorts, an implied threat. If she ignored it, would he feel impelled to go ahead and carry out his threat?

'My place is here.' Somehow she managed to keep her voice reasonably steady. 'I'm not going to run away.'

Nick straightened slowly. 'So be it.' He sounded resigned. Try as she might, Kate couldn't read anything more sinister from his tone, or from his expression. 'Just take my advice, Kate. Don't go too far from the homestead... at least, not by yourself. Make sure you always have someone with you.'

She swallowed hard and let her gaze slide away from his. Would he be warning her if he was the one she should fear?

'You're trying to frighten me,' she accused, a faint tremble in her voice. Perhaps he was still hoping she would change her mind and go. If he frightened her enough.

He caught her hand. 'No, Kate, I'm just taking precautions. Until we know what we're up against.' His glance flicked round, his hand sliding away. 'That sounds like Danny and James coming. Let's forget about it for now... I'll pour some drinks.'

Forget it? Forget that someone was striking out at her, trying to drive her from her home? Easier, far easier, said than done.

Sunday dawned, bright and crystal-clear. Kate was up early to do her chores, wanting to give herself ample time to wash her hair and change before leaving for the engagement party at Doon-gara. Even though it was a casual barbecue lunch, not a formal affair, she wanted to look her best... without delving too deeply into motives or reasons.

Since Nick's plane was only a two-seater, Danny and James set off before they did in the station ute. When Kate met Nick in front of the Big House at the allotted hour, he whistled as he ran his eyes over her, bringing a swift flush to her cheeks.

'Mmm, you don't often show off your legs,' he remarked approvingly. 'You should. They're worth showing off.'

As a change from her usual station gear of jeans or trousers, she was wearing a dress. Nothing elaborate, just a halter-top red and white spotted cotton, with a wide red belt and a skirt that flared gracefully over her hips and finished at her knees. Her mirror had told her that it flattered her slenderness and her fair colouring.

With it she wore open red sandals. No stockings, stockings would only attract grass seeds out on the airstrip. Her only jewellery was a pair of small gold earrings and a gold-rimmed red bangle round her wrist. She had been tempted to wear the gold-nugget pendant which Jeremy had given her, then prudently put it back out of sight. Nick might ask questions about it, and she was sure he'd never believe that Jeremy had simply bought it for her, the small white lie her husband had always urged her to tell if she was asked where it came from. Nick, having lived here at Ramsay Downs in the past, just might guess the truth...and that could be dangerous, in view of the other incidents that had been taking place lately. Wisest to play safe.

'You've scrubbed up well yourself,' she said lightly, running her gaze over Nick's light moleskins and tan-coloured shirt, and then, conscious of the thrust of his masculine thighs and the straining muscles under his shirt, wished she hadn't. It reminded her too forcibly of the feeling of those same thighs and muscles pressing against hers, as they had done so recently.

'I wanted to do you proud,' he said, a teasing glint in his eye.

Her gaze flickered under his. 'I'm ready to go...are you?' she asked in clipped tones, turning abruptly. If he had scrubbed up for anyone, it would be for Abigail, not for her.

The long vine-covered patio at the rear of the Stantons' home was festooned with coloured balloons and a profusion of fresh flowers, the air heavy with the scent of roses and bougainvillaea. Tables swathed in pink linen held an enticing spread of mouthwatering delicacies—colourful salads, baskets of freshly baked breads, an array of cheeses, with thick sausages and huge slabs of fresh beef waiting to be thrown on the barbecue.

The newly engaged couple, Teddy and Samantha, were obviously deliriously happy and in love. Teddy, well over six feet tall and solidly built with it, was a fresh-faced, good-humoured young man, his fiancée Samantha a slender, sweet-faced young girl with laughing brown eyes and a genuinely warm smile. Straight away Kate was confident that she need have no qualms with the two of them as her neighbours.

The celebration began well enough, with even Abigail doing her utmost to make it a happy occasion, greeting everyone, even Kate, with a dazzling smile. She looked stunning in a swirling floral skirt and a filmy gold blouse that enhanced her amber eyes and flaming red hair, and Kate was glad that she'd made the effort to wear something feminine and flattering.

She noted, with a curious dip in her spirits, the way Abigail greeted Nick with an even more dazzling smile, and a warm kiss on the lips as well, and the easy way Nick slipped his arm round the girl and drew her to one side, exchanging soft words with her. Kate felt an instant stab of jealousy, and this time she knew it wasn't prompted by mere mistrust at seeing the two with their heads together, possibly plotting against her. This was jealousy pure and simple—the green-eyed variety—and it *hurt*.

You fool, you crazy, crazy fool, she silently berated herself, but it didn't make any difference to the way she felt. She could have throttled Abigail at that moment, quite happily.

Next moment she was caught up with a group of Stanton relatives who had flown in from Brisbane for the occasion, but her gaze, almost of its own volition,

kept flickering past them to where Nick was still en-
grossed with Abigail, his dark head bowed over hers.
She felt a ridiculous spurt of relief when someone came
and plucked Abigail away from Nick, and a ripple of
something else, something that stopped the breath in her
chest, when she saw him swinging in her direction.

Touching her arm, Nick drew her over to join Teddy
and Samantha, and the four of them stood chatting for
some time, touching on one subject after another. They
talked about the state of the beef industry, about Teddy's
and Samantha's wedding plans, about books they had
read and places they had visited, and gradually Kate
found herself relaxing, enjoying the easy chatter, and
wishing it could always be like this, with Nick and herself
in perfect accord, passing time with friendly neighbours
she could relax with and enjoy... with no undercurrents
of doubt or suspicion, no painful moments, no jarring
notes to spoil their time together.

But... she hid a sigh... that was a hopeless dream,
with the ugly past persisting in casting its long
shadow... and Abigail hovering somewhere close by,
casting a very real shadow of her own.

When Teddy excused himself and headed for the barbecue to start cooking the steaks, Nick excused himself
too, to go and help. Kate, reluctant to see him go, in-
voluntarily followed him with her eyes for a second or
two, and it was only when she turned back to Samantha,
and caught the girl's whimsical gaze, that she wondered
uneasily if her eyes had revealed anything—some tell-
tale yearning, perhaps. What if Samantha, quite inno-
cently, passed on her observations to Abigail?

'Sam, I think Uncle John wants to speak to you...'
It was Abigail's voice, sending Kate's heart fluttering to

her toes. As Samantha smilingly flitted away, Abigail tugged Kate to one side.

'My dear, I've just heard about your troubles. It's appalling! Have you any idea...?'

Kate shook her head. Who had mentioned it? Nick? Danny? James? What did it matter? You couldn't hush up trouble like that. Not for long—and especially not out here in the outback.

'You haven't?' Abigail pursed her bright red lips. 'Well, of course, men hate working for a woman. It could be any one of them, couldn't it?'

Kate's eyes widened, then narrowed. 'You think it's someone who *works* for me?'

'Well, who else?' Abigail shrugged. 'Of course, it might not even *be* a man. How's... Minya settling back in?'

'Minya?' Kate stared at her. 'No, that's impossible.' But was it? Minya, more than anyone, must want to see Nick take over as sole owner of Ramsay Downs. She frowned, and heaved a sigh. Possible or not, she didn't want to believe that of Minya—or of any of her employees, for that matter. 'I did wonder,' she admitted slowly, 'if maybe Leif Clancy——'

'Leif Clancy?' Abigail gave a dismissive laugh. 'Hardly! One of our stockmen was up at Longreach this week. Leif's in hospital with a broken leg. He's been there for the past week!'

'Oh.' Kate felt a coldness creeping over her. If Leif Clancy was in the clear, then who...? Could Abigail possibly be right? That it was someone who worked for her? Someone who resented her presence at Ramsay Downs, and wanted to undermine her confidence so that she would give up and go away?

The one who resented her the most, who most wanted her gone, was...

She shivered.

'What's wrong, Kate? You've gone quite pale.' Abigail's hand touched her arm, her slender fingers cool on her skin. 'You're letting this get you down, my dear, aren't you? Not that I blame you. It must be terribly disheartening knowing everyone's against you. If I were in your place I'd have given up long ago.'

Kate shifted restlessly, wanting to escape, but Abigail had steered her into a leafy corner of the veranda, making ready escape impossible. 'I can't imagine why you persist in carrying on, Kate, with so much stacked against you,' Abigail persisted. 'It's not as if there's no one else capable of running the place. You know Nick's more than capable of taking over...of carrying out your precious Jeremy's dream, as you call it.'

The mention of Nick, and the reminder of Jeremy in the same breath, especially the derisive way Abigail referred to Jeremy's dream, were too much for Kate.

'How do I know Nick's not the one who's behind all those——?' She stopped, clapping a hand to her mouth. She could have bitten her tongue out. Now her suspicions were out in the open...the suspicions she hadn't wanted to face up to, hadn't wanted to believe, wasn't certain she *did* believe. And now Abigail knew...

She felt like groaning aloud. 'Then again,' she added hastily, knowing it was too late, that the damage was done, 'it could be anyone who works for me, as you say. I'll just have to be more...more vigilant,' she finished lamely.

'Kate, come with me.' Abigail's tone was purposeful as her fingers closed round Kate's arm, dragging her from the patio deep into the garden, away from prying ears.

'You can't blame Nick for feeling resentful,' the girl said earnestly. 'He does have a claim...you know that as well as I do.'

Kate's eyes widened. Abigail wasn't making any attempt to deny that Nick might have been responsible for those incidents. Did *she* believe it too? And *condone* it?

'He has no claim at all!' She shook the girl's hand from her arm. 'He lost any rights he ever had long ago! If it's Nick Ramsay who's been doing all these things, hoping I'll leave, then he's grossly miscalculated. I would never hand the place over to him—never!'

Strangely, as the words left her lips, she heard the hollowness in her voice, as if she was repeating a well worn refrain. Didn't she really mean it any more? Didn't she truly believe that Nick could be responsible for those malicious incidents? Or was it simply that she didn't *want* to believe it?

'Kate, what do you mean—Nick has lost all his rights?' Abigail frowned into her face. 'You mean because Jeremy married *you*? Kate, you only married into the Ramsay name—Nick was *born* a Ramsay. Don't you feel guilty that you're denying Nick what by rights should be his now? Nick's done so much to get the place back on its feet. Why won't you step aside now, as he wants you to do, and hand the place over to him?'

Kate inhaled deeply. 'You must know why.' Her voice throbbed with emotion. 'Because he doesn't deserve it! Not after what he did to Jeremy. He hated and persecuted Jeremy all their lives. He—he did his best to destroy him. Out of jealousy and—and sheer greed!'

Abigail stared at her. 'What on earth are you talking about, Kate? It was Jeremy who hated and persecuted *Nick*, not the other way round. Jeremy did some pretty despicable things to Nick over the years. He was always jealous of Nick, from the moment Nick was born. He even blamed Nick for his mother's death. He was always throwing it up at him.'

Kate's body had stiffened in shock. 'No, that's not—— You're saying *Jeremy* was the one who... Oh, that's ridiculous! Why would Jeremy be jealous of Nick? Jeremy was Logan Ramsay's own son—his own flesh and blood, the son he adored. Logan only tolerated Nick because he felt he owed it to his wife to look after him.'

Abigail gave a snort. 'Nick was much loved, Kate, not just tolerated. They all loved him. His mother, before she died, Minya, even Logan Ramsay himself, despite the fact that Nick wasn't his real son, despite the fact that Nick was the son of his wife's lover! They all adored Nick! He was everyone's favourite. I must say I felt rather sorry for Jeremy at times. I think I would have felt jealous too, in his place.'

Kate shook her head, feeling as if she were stumbling around in a kind of fog. It couldn't be true. *Jeremy* had been the favourite son. Jeremy... Logan Ramsay's blue-eyed, golden-haired, much cherished son. Jeremy himself had told her how cherished he had been, and she had never had any reason to doubt him.

'You expect me to believe that *Nick* was the favourite son?' she scoffed. 'Logan sent Nick away in disgrace! And after he'd gone, Logan got rid of every last photograph of Nick in the house! He couldn't stand being reminded of him!'

'He got rid of——?' Abigail blinked at her. 'Kate, that's simply not true. I saw those photographs of Nick...many times. If they're not there now, then Jeremy must have got rid of them himself after his father died. Knowing him, it would have been the first thing he'd think of!'

Kate gulped and bit her lip, recalling with a quiver of unease that Jeremy, at the time of his father's death, had gone back to Ramsay Downs ahead of her. He had wanted to sort things out, he'd said, prepare the house for her. No, she thought wildly. Jeremy would never...

'Why would Logan Ramsay prefer Nick, the child of his wife's lover, over his own son?' she demanded scathingly. 'His own flesh and blood! That's crazy!'

Abigail jerked a shoulder. 'I guess because he was so like Logan's wife Sophie... Nick's mother. His nature, looks, everything. Logan adored her...and whether you like it or not, Kate, he adored Nick too.'

'Nick tried to *kill* Jeremy,' Kate burst out. 'Oh, I know they were only boys at the time, but that doesn't excuse it. Nick cold-bloodedly told Jeremy that his father needed him, and that Jeremy was to ride out to meet him, on Sinbad, their new stallion—knowing full well that Sinbad was vicious, not fit to be ridden, and far too dangerous for a young lad to handle. Jeremy could have been killed that day. It was only his skill on a horse that saved him.'

'Oh, Kate...' Abigail shook her head pityingly. 'It was Jeremy who sent *Nick* out on Sinbad that day—Jeremy obviously twisted the story around, like everything else. It's true, Kate. We all heard about it. Jeremy was obviously hoping that Nick would fall off and break his neck. And it could easily have happened...Nick was only a young kid at the time.'

Kate drew in a fractured breath. 'If that's true, then why did Logan send *Nick* away in disgrace? Why not banish Jeremy?'

'I dare say because Logan wanted to keep Jeremy under his wing, where he could keep an eye on him, and if possible straighten him out. And you must remember, Kate, Jeremy was the elder son, and would take over

Ramsay Downs one day. Logan was keen for Nick to learn other skills, in other areas...he knew the two would never be able to work together at Ramsay Downs. He sent Nick away for his own good...but, most of all, it was for his own *safety*. Oh, Logan made sure Nick was well provided for—always. Nick never lost out.'

Kate's hand fluttered in the air. 'But—but what about the time Nick set fire to their barn? The barn where they kept all their valuable machinery? Nick went as far as planting evidence so that Jeremy would get the blame...but, luckily for Jeremy, someone saw Nick and reported back to Logan.'

Abigail gave a snort. 'Is that what Jeremy told you?' Her mouth curved, almost admiringly. 'Nick didn't start that fire, Kate—Jeremy did. *He* planted that evidence. And yes, there was an eye-witness—but it was Jeremy who was caught out, not Nick. One of the stockmen came forward afterwards and cleared Nick. There was an enormous stink when the truth came out. We heard about it from one of our stockmen. Logan was furious with Jeremy. For Nick's own good, he packed poor old Nick off again—for good this time. Not because he wanted Nick to go, but because he was worried that Jeremy would end up doing Nick some real harm some day.'

Kate's shoulders slumped. She was stunned, not daring to believe that it could be true. 'If Jeremy hated his brother so much,' she said slowly, seizing on something else, 'doesn't it strike you as odd that he'd run and fetch his mother that time when Nick fell into the dam? Why not simply leave him there to drown?'

Abigail didn't turn a hair. 'Nick was just a toddler at the time, unable to swim,' she said dismissively. 'No doubt Jeremy thought it was already too late to save him. Or maybe he saw his mother coming looking for them and thought he'd better start yelling for help or she'd wonder afterwards why he hadn't. Kate, what you obviously don't know is that Jeremy pushed Nick into the dam in the first place!'

Kate's hand clutched at her throat. 'How—how could you possibly know that? Jeremy's mother drowned that day. You don't expect me to believe that Jeremy told you that himself? Or are you saying that Nick told you?'

'Minya told me, Kate—only recently, as a matter of fact, while she was working for us. She heard it from Nick himself, after she'd dragged him from the dam. A child that young would hardly be likely to lie about a thing like that. Minya made Nick keep quiet about it. She was afraid of what the consequences might be if it came out, that it might somehow rebound on Nick. With his mother dead, and with Nick not being Logan's real son... Well, you can't blame her, can you, for wanting to hush up the truth?'

A wave of light-headedness swept over Kate. Rallying, she demanded, 'If everything you've told me is true, why didn't Nick tell me the truth himself when I threw Jeremy's accusations at him? That seems to suggest, wouldn't you say, that you've got the facts all wrong?' Unless Abigail had twisted the story around deliberately. Being the wronged first wife, she would have no cause to be loyal to Jeremy's memory. And she now clearly had her sights set on Nick Ramsay. And no doubt on Ramsay Downs as well.

Abigail shook her head. 'You can't know Nick very well, Kate. He's a proud man. I could never imagine him going crawling to any woman. Especially if he knows he's in the right. Look, ask Minya if you're still in any doubt. Ask my parents, or anyone who was around in those days. Jeremy was lying to you, Kate. He hated and resented Nick, and he was obsessed with stopping Nick ever inheriting Ramsay Downs. You must have been aware of that, at the very least. Why don't you face up to it, Kate? Jeremy treated Nick appallingly, and here's your chance to make amends. Ramsay Downs should by rights go to Nick now. It's what Logan Ramsay would have wanted.'

As Kate was trying to absorb all this, a call came from the house, penetrating through the fog of her thoughts. 'Abigail! Are you out there? We want to drink a toast. Are you coming?'

'Coming, Mother.' Abigail glanced at Kate with a wry smile. 'I can see you're finding all this a bit hard to take in, Kate. Jeremy obviously did a good job on you. But believe me, it's all true. If you won't face Nick with it—and I can understand that you'd be wary of accepting his side of things—then why not speak to Minya? She'll tell you the truth. She was right there when it all happened.'

'Will she?' Kate had her doubts about that. Minya adored Nick. She'd be likely to say anything to advance his cause.

On the other hand, would the elderly housekeeper be brave enough to tell the truth—assuming Jeremy was indeed the villain of the piece? Brave enough to tell Jeremy's widow, who also happened to be her employer, that her late husband had been a jealous, vindictive liar!

Kate sighed tremulously. How would she herself ever be able to come to terms with it, if what Abigail had told her about Jeremy was true? The whole of her brief two-year marriage to Jeremy would have been based on lies and deception. The golden-haired husband who she had always believed had been victimised by his malevolent brother would himself have been responsible for every evil deed he had ever placed at his despised brother's feet!

Kate followed Abigail back to the house with dragging footsteps. 'Jeremy obviously did a good job on you,' Abigail had said. Nick had once used similar words, she remembered with growing unease. Something about her husband brainwashing her. If all that Abigail had told her about Jeremy was true, how was she ever going to live with it?

'You might ask Minya about that bracelet she was supposed to have stolen from you too,' was Abigail's parting shot. 'She swore black and blue that someone had *planted* it in her room.' Her red lips twisted. 'Just Jeremy's style!'

Kate almost stumbled. Abigail had put into words a possibility she had long wondered about but had stubbornly resisted facing up to.

'Why would he want to do that?' she asked faintly, with a sinking feeling inside.

'Easiest way to get rid of her, I imagine,' Abigail threw back. 'He and Minya were never exactly bosom buddies. And to keep her away from *you*,' she added shrewdly. 'With Minya there, you just might have found out there was a side of him he'd rather you didn't know about.'

Kate couldn't answer, her eyelids fluttering down over her eyes.

'Poor Kate,' said Abigail, pausing. 'You still can't believe it, can you? Why don't you ask my parents? They always knew what Jeremy was like, how jealous he was of Nick. They never liked poor Jeremy, even when I defied everyone and married him. They made an effort, for my sake, but they were glad when we got divorced.'

'Why *did* you marry him?' Kate asked curiously. 'If all you say is true?'

'Birds of a feather, I guess.' Abigail gave a self-mocking smile. 'And he did have a certain...style and charm about him. You, Kate, of all people must agree. He swept *you* off your feet, didn't he?'

Without waiting for an answer she swung away, hips swaying, auburn curls bouncing.

Kate wasn't sure how she got through the rest of the day. She couldn't concentrate on a thing anyone said, could only pick at her food, hardly drank a drop of the Stantons' fine champagne, knowing her mind was already in a daze and that if she drank too much she would never be able to think, and she found it impossible to meet Nick in the eye, so kept out of his way as much as she could.

All she could concentrate on were the thoughts seething through her head, going back over everything Abigail had told her, over everything Jeremy had ever told her, and over the little Nick had volunteered himself. And by the time Nick was ready to leave, voicing anxiety about being away from Ramsay Downs for too long, she knew in her heart that she couldn't simply ignore Abigail's story, couldn't dismiss it out of hand as merely the spiteful fabrication of a rejected wife. She had to find out the truth, no matter how much it cost, how much it hurt. She owed it to Nick...and to her own peace of mind.

This was hardly the time to approach the Stantons. Not here, with all these people around, and not today of all days. She would, she resolved, start with Minya.

She knew that Nick was the one she ought to face, but something, a deep-seated caution, held her back. It was just possible that Abigail might after all have been lying, deliberately twisting things around, and, if she gave Nick the chance, he might seize on the story and turn it to his advantage, in his desperation to get his hands on Ramsay Downs. It seemed highly suspect that Nick had never volunteered this version of events himself, badly as he wanted Ramsay Downs. Proud man or not, there had to be a better reason than mere pride holding him back. Perhaps... because it simply wasn't true?

And there was something else too that was holding her back. The fact that there was someone out there—and it was evident now that it couldn't be Leif Clancy—who was maliciously causing trouble for her, obviously trying to dishearten her and drive her away. And the person with the most to gain had to be... Nick himself.

Even if Abigail had told her the truth and Nick had never been the monster that Jeremy had made him out to be, there was still the possibility that Nick, frustrated at being denied his inheritance and resentful at what Jeremy had done to him over the years and by what Jeremy's widow was now trying to take from him, felt justified in using any underhand means at his disposal to drive her out and claim his inheritance.

Which would mean that Nick had turned into the very monster that Jeremy had always made him out to be! And in that case, he wouldn't deserve to have even a share!

Kate sighed heavily. Oh, Nick, if it is you doing those horrible things... why, oh, why, instead of lashing out in spite, or hurt, or whatever... instead of using hurtful, underhand methods to try to drive me out, why didn't you simply tell me the truth, and appeal to my sense of justice?

She felt her heart squeeze in pain. Because Abigail's version wasn't the truth at all?

Until she knew without a shadow of doubt what the truth was and who was behind those vicious incidents, she simply couldn't afford to let down her guard...couldn't afford to trust Nick. To trust *anyone*.

Despite the doubts that were still rampaging through her, she felt her heart twist painfully as she followed Nick from the house, her eyes misting as she watched the familiar swing of his stride, the slight roll of his hips, the way his rumpled black hair ruffled in the breeze.

Was her heart twisting for Nick, or for the man she had married, the husband she had never truly known? she wondered, tormented by a riot of agonising, conflicting emotions.

CHAPTER EIGHT

'IS THERE something on your mind, Kate?' Nick shouted over the noise of the engine as the plane swooped into the air. 'You seem distracted.'

She wasn't facing him, and jumped as she felt his fingers close over the hands clasped in her lap. She tensed at his touch, but didn't withdraw them. She was tempted for a second to burst out with the questions uppermost in her mind, but she caught them back in time. She had made up her mind to wait, to speak to Minya first. After that...well, she would see. Besides, she was far too confused and emotional just now, her mind too racked by the doubts Abigail had planted there. Doubts...about Jeremy, her husband. She needed time to think, to throw her mind back over the past, over the time they had spent together, to see if she could find any answers of her own.

'You're worrying about what might be happening back home?' Nick's voice broke into the silence.

She seized on the excuse, asking warily, 'You think I have reason to be worried?'

There was a faint pause before he answered. 'I hope not, but I admit, I'll be glad to get home myself.'

Home, he kept saying. Was he thinking of it as his home or hers?

She closed her eyes, a bitter despair washing over her. One thing she knew; it could never be *their* home...together, in partnership of any kind. Whatever the truth turned out to be. Even if Nick turned out to be the paragon of virtue that Abigail had made him out to be, there was no point in dreaming of any kind of future with Nick—with or without Abigail making her own play for him. Nick would have even more reason to resent her. She was his brother's widow...the brother who had made his life a misery and driven him away from his home and his family.

No wonder he had always been so anxious for her to leave!

Nobody felt like dinner after the feast of food at the Stantons', and when Minya offered to prepare a light snack of sandwiches instead Kate declined and fled to her room, supposedly to catch up on her correspondence, but in reality so that she could be alone. When she finally fell into bed, exhausted and emotionally drained, she couldn't sleep, restlessly going over and over the past two years in her mind, struggling to accept that the dashing, golden-haired man she had married, the man she had thought she loved—if she truly *had* loved him, would she be having doubts now?—could well have been lying to her all along, deliberately distorting everything he had ever told her about himself and about Nick, giving a false impression of his brother to make himself look good in her eyes, the hard-done-by older brother, and she knew she would never have any peace of mind until she knew the truth.

She waited until she saw Nick drive off in the jeep with James the next morning to dig up and repair the damaged windmill, before seizing her chance to speak to Minya in the kitchen, where the Aboriginal woman was baking bread. Kate often helped with the baking, and as they worked side by side she said brightly, as if out of the blue, 'I'm glad you agreed to come back to us, Minya.'

She saw the woman's dark hands pause on the dough she was kneading, and added, without waiting for comment, 'I'm sure Nick's glad too. You're very fond of him, aren't you, Minya?'

'Nick's a good man, real good.' Minya's bony chin jutted in faint defiance. 'It's good he's come back. Where he belong.'

Kate took a deep breath. 'You've known him all his life, haven't you, Minya? From a baby.'

'Mm—long time.'

'He was lucky he had you there when his mother died. It must have been difficult for him—since he wasn't Logan Ramsay's real son.'

The small black eyes snapped round. 'Mr Logan, he love Nick like a son. Never cared about him bein' me cousin Kim's son, not his. Mr Logan always crazy about Missus Sophie—even after what she done.'

Kate moistened her lips with the tip of her tongue. There was the ring of truth in Minya's rasping voice. So Nick had been loved! Why, she reflected poignantly, have I never thought to ask these questions before? She sighed, knowing the answer to that. Until now, she had never thought to question what Jeremy had told her... it was as simple as that.

'Missus Sophie never meant to hurt Mr Logan,' Minya asserted gruffly. 'She very much younger, see, and she got lonely with him away so much. And Kim...Kim was a good-lookin' feller—ladies' man. Always told him he'd get into trouble one day if he didn't watch out.'

'Kim's death must have been...a terrible shock to Sophie,' Kate pressed on as Minya lapsed into a brooding silence.

The woman shrugged her bony shoulders. 'Missus Sophie never held what Mr Logan done against him.

She knew it was an accident. Mr Logan felt real bad. When Nick was born, he loved him like his own son.'

'And how did . . . Jeremy feel about that?' Kate asked carefully.

Minya's black gaze slid away.

'Minya?'

'You mean he never told you?'

'Told me . . . what, Minya?'

'How much he hated Nick.'

Kate grew still. 'You're saying the two boys hated each other?'

'I'm sayin' Jeremy hated Nick. Never stopped hating him.'

'And what about Nick?'

'Nick never hated nobody,' said Minya firmly.

Kate swallowed. 'Did Jeremy ever try to . . . hurt Nick, Minya?'

Minya started thumping the dough on the bench, avoiding Kate's eye.

'Minya, I know what happened the day Nick's mother drowned. I just want to hear it from you.'

Minya slid a look upward. 'You mean you know about Jeremy pushing Nick into the dam? Jeremy *told* you?'

Kate gasped. Not 'Abigail told you', not 'Nick told you', both of which might have been suspect. But 'Jeremy told you'. . . It couldn't have been more damning.

She gulped, and said with a shake of her head, 'Jeremy told me they never got on. Minya, did Nick ever try to . . . hit back at Jeremy for what he had done? I imagine there must have been times when . . . when they both hit out at each other?'

Minya's head jerked back. 'Nick never . . . it was Jeremy who . . .' She was becoming agitated now. 'What lies did Jeremy tell you?' she demanded.

'Lies, Minya?'

Something seemed to snap in Minya, and a torrent of words burst from her lips. 'Nick had plenty reason to hit back at Jeremy, but Nick, he never hurt nobody— Nick a good feller, real good, you ask anyone. But Jeremy... that boy got a wicked heart. Black enough to send Nick out on a crazy stallion. Wicked enough to burn down a barn and try to put the blame on Nick. And plenty more the boss never got to hear about. Jeremy drove Nick out of his home and now you—you're trying to do the——' She stopped, her body rigid with shock, appalled at what she had almost said.

Kate let out a deep, shuddering sigh. 'It's all right, Minya, it's all right. I know now... I didn't before... Calm yourself, Minya. I'll make it up to Nick. I promise!'

By mid-afternoon Kate had decided what she was going to do. It was a compromise rather than a solution, but she owed Nick that much, at least. And it was just possible that what she intended to offer him was all he had ever wanted, or hoped for, right from the start.

She summoned James and Danny and sent them off in the ute to the local town on the pretext of picking up some provisions, suggesting that, as it was getting late, they might as well stay there overnight and make a night of it. She had no trouble persuading them.

Then she asked Minya to prepare a special dinner for two on the veranda, and she spent a full hour before dinner pampering herself, brushing her hair until it shone, refreshing her face with a cooling mask, taking particular care with her make-up, enhancing the green of her eyes with shadow and brushing mascara on to her lashes, then outlining her lips with pencil before applying a brighter-than-usual lipstick. She chose a green silk blouse that Nick hadn't seen before, and, instead of wearing trousers as she usually did in the evenings, she chose a cream wool skirt and gold sandals.

Just before going down to meet Nick, she took her jewel box from the drawer of her dressing-table and plucked out her gold-nugget pendant, which she hadn't worn since Jeremy died.

As she drew the thin chain round her neck and clasped it at her nape, she felt the weight, the coldness of the gold nugget against her bare skin, and swallowed, knowing what her decision could mean. Nick could be gone by tomorrow... gone out of her life for good.

She felt a moment of painful indecision as she stood gazing at her image in the mirror, her gaze dwelling for a moment on the gleaming gold nugget at her throat, then flickering upward to meet the pensive green eyes staring back at her. How could she bear to see him go out of her life?

But she had made up her mind and there was no turning back now. She swung round and headed for the door, feeling her heart quicken its beat as she heard another door bang and knew that Nick had arrived.

As she stepped out on to the veranda, her eyes, wide and apprehensive, met his.

'Well... you didn't tell me this was a special occasion.' Nick's eyes softened as they held hers for a long moment. Her heart slowly turned over, and she stared back, noting the tiny pinpricks of light in the depthless black eyes, the length of his eyelashes, the way his eyebrows almost met at the bridge of his nose, as if she were seeing him for the first time in her life. And she was, in a way. She was seeing the real Nick, without any misconceptions clouding her vision, seeing him as she should have seen him all along, as she had, in her deepest heart of hearts, already begun to see him, even with Jeremy's lies still niggling at the back of her mind.

She didn't know what to say. Her mouth felt suddenly dry, and she felt a tightness in her chest. What if he didn't notice the pendant, or if he did notice, failed to realise its significance?

She dismissed the thought with a trembling sigh. What difference did it make? She would simply have to tell him.

'You look wonderful,' he said finally, breaking eye contact to let his gaze wander down her flushed cheeks, along the smooth line of her jaw, down the slender curve of her throat. And then his entire body seemed to freeze as his eyes fastened on the gold nugget.

'Where did you get this?' His tone was sharp as he reached out and slipped his hand underneath it, the touch of his fingers on her throat burning like fire.

Kate gulped. There was a dangerous glint in Nick's black eyes. It was hard to tell if it was anger, excitement or greed. She was aware of a twinge of disappointment. What had she been expecting, for heaven's sake? Apathy? Indifference? She found her voice. 'Jeremy gave it to me. He... found it.'

'Found it *where*?' He was peering into her face now, his eyes like ice, his tone as cold.

She took a deep breath. 'He found it up in—up in that far north corner, where Logan's father was...killed.'

Nick let the pendant drop, a cold weight on her skin. His breath hissed out through his teeth. 'So there *is* gold up there! And Jeremy could barely wait for his father's body to grow cold before high-tailing it up there to get his hands on it. Hell, Kate, why didn't you tell me about this before?'

She stared up at him wordlessly, her eyes pained, wanting to retort, Because Jeremy told me not to tell anyone, least of all you. And it seems he had good reason. The gold *is* all you want... why else would you be getting so excited? It was only her sense of justice, the realisation that Nick deserved some recompense for what Jeremy had done to him, that strangled the words in her throat.

'I suppose Jeremy told you to keep quiet about it.' Nick's mouth twisted, his voice harsh with contempt. 'When did he find it?'

Kate said dully, 'Just a few weeks before he was killed. He—he found the nugget with a—with a metal detector, he said. He was up there just fossicking around. He intended going back at the end of the polo season to—to do some deeper excavating, but he—he never had the chance.'

'Thank God for that!' Nick thrust his face closer to hers, his black eyes hard, burning into her face. 'Now you listen to me, Kate. Logan Ramsay never touched that gold. And you're not to either!'

Kate paled. She said hoarsely, eyeing him scathingly, 'Oh, don't worry, Nick Ramsay, I'm not going to take it away from you. It's all yours. I trust it will be enough to satisfy you!'

Something shimmered in the black eyes. 'What do you mean, it's all mine?'

'Just what I say. I...' She hesitated, pain twisting inside her. 'If that's all you want then you can have it. I guess I owe you that much.'

The dark eyebrows rose a fraction. 'You... *owe* me?'

She moistened her lips. 'For what Jeremy did to you. Nick, why didn't you tell me the truth?' she burst out. 'That it was Jeremy who did all those horrible things in

the past, not you. That he was the one who was jealous
and filled with hate.'

There was a long, tense pause. 'Who told you?' Nick
asked at length.

She tried to read what was in his face, but it was like
stone, giving nothing away. 'Does it matter?' she whispered. 'The fact is, I know. I know the truth at last. Oh,
Nick, why did you let me go on thinking the worst of
you? Why didn't you tell me?'

'Would you have wanted to hear?'

'Nick, of course I——' She broke off, chewing her lip,
her eyes narrowing. 'Was it ... just to save my feelings,
Nick? Because you didn't want me thinking badly of my
husband?'

He didn't answer immediately. Then ... 'Something
like that. Why ruin your illusions? You obviously
thought the sun shone from Jeremy.'

Had she? Kate stared at him obliquely, frowning. Then
she gave herself a tiny shake and said, 'But you must
have known I'd find out eventually.' Or had he hoped
she'd be gone before long, so why bother? She must remember that he had been anxious right from the beginning for her to sell up and leave; he'd made no secret
of the fact that he wanted Ramsay Downs for himself.
Only yesterday he had still been urging her to go, citing
those vicious attacks on her as a reason, and pretending
that he was concerned for her safety.

Had he been only pretending? Her heart squeezed with
a vague, illogical hope. She had told him time and time
again that she was definitely staying, and yet Nick was
still here, still helping her in every way he could. Why?
Was he still hanging on to the hope that if he played his
cards right she would give up in the end and go? Or was
something else keeping him here?

Abigail, perhaps.

Or even . . .

She flicked her tongue over her lips, not daring to complete that second, wildly improbable thought. There was one thing at least that she could find out.

'Nick, I meant what I said just now. I want you to have that piece of land up north—and any gold that goes with it. It's all yours, Nick. It's what you want, isn't it?'

Instead of the acceptance she had expected, his eyes burned into hers, scorching her with his contempt. 'You think I want that land because of the *gold*?'

She blinked at him. 'Well, d-don't you?'

'No, I damn well do not!'

'Then why?' she whispered. Her eyes clouding, she asked painfully, 'Just to stop me having it?'

'If it means I'd be doing that, yes.'

She felt her heart shrivelling. 'You still resent me that much?' she whispered. 'Is this your way of hitting back at Jeremy for what he did to you? By hitting out at me?'

'No!' He reached for her, grabbing her by the shoulders and giving her a shake. 'Dear heaven, Kate, when will you stop thinking the worst of me?'

'Well, why *do* you want that land?' She looked at him in confusion. 'You expect me to believe it's pure sentiment? Because your grandfather—a man you never knew, never met—was born there? Nick, you never even met your real father! So *why*, Nick?'

His hands slid away. 'Let's have a drink.' As he turned aside, he asked impassively, 'Were you speaking the truth when you said you'd never been up there yourself?'

She threw him an indignant look. 'Yes! Of course it was the truth.'

'Then I must take you up there some time.'

Her heart gave an extra beat. Why would he want her to go up there with him? 'It's wild country, Nick. There'd be nowhere for a plane to land.'

'I'm aware of that. We'll drive up.'

'But it would take all day!'

'So we'll take all day.' As he fell silent, attending to the drinks, Kate found herself wondering why Jeremy had never taken her up there himself. He'd told her he hadn't wanted to attract any undue attention to the region, that it might arouse suspicion. But now she began to wonder if that was the only reason, the real reason.

Nick handed her a glass of wine, and raised his own. 'Let's drink to...' he paused, an ironic smile touching his lips, 'openness and...a new beginning. Mmm?' The eyes that came to rest on hers were fathomless black pools, tiny flickers of light glowing deep within. What was he thinking, feeling, at this moment? she wondered, searching the glittering black depths, in vain, for a clue.

'I'll drink to that.' She touched her glass to his. 'And to something else. To truth...and justice,' she said firmly.

His eyes held hers. 'You don't owe me anything, Kate.'

'Yes, well...' Did he truly believe that? Or was he just saying it now that he knew he had the gold? But...her eyes fluttered away in confusion. He didn't *want* the gold. He'd said so. What else could be out there?

Uranium? She pursed her lips. No, Nick would never...

'What's this?' Nick had moved over to the small table Minya had set up for their dinner with the best silver and glassware. He was looking down at the centrepiece, a bowl of pink-tipped cream roses, which Kate herself had picked and placed there. He touched a delicate petal with his finger. 'Peace,' he commented in a low voice, and turned to face her, raising a quizzical eyebrow. 'Is that significant? You chose them, Kate?'

She nodded, pleased that he'd noticed, and understood. When he smiled, a disarming smile that sent her heart into a wild spin, she smiled back, all her defences melting away. The tension between them melted away at the same time, and they settled down to talk about station matters. It was only later, as they were relaxing with coffee at the end of their meal, that Jeremy's name resurfaced.

'I'm sorry, Kate, that you had to find out about...what happened in the past,' Nick said quietly. 'But you must try to keep it in perspective. It was something between Jeremy and me—between two half-brothers who never got on. It needn't affect you, or your memories of Jeremy. He twisted things around because he loved you and——'

'He *lied* to me,' Kate cut in, her voice husky with hurt anger. 'If people truly love each other, they don't lie to each other.'

'If he lied to you about the past, Kate, it would have been because he loved you and didn't want the events of the past distorting the way you saw him. Look, forget about what he did to me. Remember him as he was when *you* knew him. You loved each other, didn't you? Hold on to that, and forget what happened before you knew him.'

'But it wasn't only you and the past that he lied about,' Kate said in a strangled voice. 'He lied about his health, he lied about Minya stealing from us, he lied about why he broke up with Abigail, he lied about the reason he was so desperate for a child, and he made me feel guilty for not getting pregnant, when he was the one who——' Her voice broke, and she dropped her head in her hands.

Nick came swiftly round the table and drew her to her feet, holding her against him, her head cradled against his shoulder. 'Kate, don't distress yourself...please! I'm sorry, I'm truly sorry. If he lied to you, it would have been because he wanted to be something to you that he felt he wasn't... because he loved you so much that he——'

'*Did* he?' She looked up at him with a haunted sadness in her eyes. 'Sometimes I wonder if he ever really loved me at all, and if I...ever loved him. I certainly never really knew him!' she said bitterly. 'It's funny,' she added pensively, searching for the right words. 'I'm starting to see it all so clearly now. I was in love with romance, I think...with a fantasy figure rather than a real man. When I married Jeremy I'd never been in love before, you see, and I—I had nothing to compare it with. When Jeremy made love to me, it never... I mean, I thought that what I felt was enough, until——' She choked off the rest in dismay, realising what she had almost given away.

She felt Nick's heartbeat hammering unevenly against her ear. 'Until what, Kate?' she heard him ask softly. 'Until another man made you feel more? Is that what you're trying to say?'

She stirred in his arms, her cheeks burning. How could she have said what she had, when she was still confused by so many unanswered questions, when there was still Abigail...when there was still somebody out there who...?

She felt a cold shiver glide down her spine.

'You're cold.' She felt his hand move over her shoulderblade, gently rubbing the tense muscles. And then she felt his body stiffen. 'What the——?'

Her head jerked up. Nick was looking past her, out across the yard. She turned her head to follow his gaze—and bit back a gasp.

'Nick, what is it? A bushfire?' An ominous red glow was clearly visible in the night sky, way out beyond the home paddocks.

'At this time of year? And with no wind?' He came suddenly to life, releasing her abruptly. 'It looks like the drafting yards! I'll grab the jeep and get out there . . . I'll take Smithy with me. Find the rest of the guys, will you, and send them out with the water truck?' He was already halfway to the door.

'Nick, be careful!' Kate called after him.

He paused just long enough to flash her a smile. Then he was gone.

CHAPTER NINE

As THE water truck lurched into the drafting yards, Kate screwed up her eyes against the bright dazzle of flames roaring into the night sky.

'The round yard's on fire!' she gasped, staring in dismay at the huge circular sorting pen which Nick had built for her. The seven-foot-tall timber supports and all six gates were ablaze, a raging inferno, and, as the men yanked at the hoses and started pouring water on to the flames, she stumbled round looking for Nick.

'Kate, what in hell's name are you doing here? Get back!' roared Nick, and she gasped in protest as a vice-like grip swung her round and almost sent her sprawling.

As she staggered back, she yelled back in hurt fury, 'Don't you manhandle me, Nick Ramsay! I've every right to be here!' She heard the rising hysteria in her voice and recognised it as sheer panic. Panic at the thought that someone was still striking out at her, still wanting to drive her away, panic at not knowing who it was, panic at the thought that maybe she didn't, after all, have any right to be here, not any more. And it was that thought that made her panic most of all, the thought of having to leave here, of having to leave *Nick* ...

A deafening crash brought her head round sharply, her eyes flying wide as the blazing timber posts gave way and crashed to the ground in a formidable shower of sparks and hot licking flames. She saw Nick's figure outlined against the bright glow, spinning back out of danger just in time, and she caught her breath, realising with a rush of intense, choking emotion why he had pushed her away.

Without even thinking, she stumbled forward and threw herself at him, clinging to his arm, her shocked eyes searching his ash-blackened face. 'Nick, Nick, are you all right?'

His warm strong hand closed over hers, clasping it tight, and as he dragged her away he stared down into her face, his eyes like black hot coal in the fierce orange glow, a red light glowing deep within them.

'Sure, I'm fine, Kate. It's bad luck about the round yard, but it could have been a lot worse. We could have had cattle in there.'

She shuddered, and he must have felt the tremor run through her, because he said in a voice that she found almost unbearably tender, 'It'll be all right, it'll be all right.' He wrapped his arms round her and crushed her against him. 'Nothing else is going to happen, Kate...I'll make sure of that.'

She sighed, feeling deliciously warm and safe in his arms, and strangely languorous too, her nerve ends springing to exquisite life at his closeness. At the same time he made her feel that she could believe him. She wanted to believe him, wanted it more than anything in the world—and yet how could he be so sure that nothing more would happen, unless...? Her eyes clouded with uncertainty. Unless, after all, he was responsible for the things that kept happening...or knew who was. Had he guessed that she was in a weakened state right now, teetering on the verge of handing everything over to him, and felt there was no longer any need to frighten her into leaving, now that he had her where he had always wanted her?

'You don't believe me, Kate?'

She felt a prickling warmth in her cheeks, conscious that he was still staring down at her, the planes and bones of his face eerily illuminated in the fiery glow, his black brows drawn, casting his eyes into deep shadow, hiding whatever expression was there.

'If you say so, Nick, then I believe you,' she said, swallowing hard. She felt a deep pang of guilt that she could still harbour any doubts about him at all, now that she knew the truth about the past. Nick had once accused her of being brainwashed by Jeremy, and here she was, still thinking the worst of him, still thinking of him as the man Jeremy had falsely made him out to be. And he wasn't, she knew that now...time and time again she had seen the good in Nick, even during the time she had still been influenced by Jeremy's lies. The unfairness of it made her want to shrivel up in shame.

'Hey, Nick, take a look at this! Here's where your fire started!' shouted Smithy, and Nick let her go and stepped away, leaving her alone, feeling suddenly chilled, bereft. Giving herself a tiny shake, she followed him over to where Smithy's flashlight was illuminating a pile of ashes and charred logs near the base of the crumbling round yard.

'Whoever it was meant business,' drawled Smithy. 'They've poured kerosene around too, I reckon, to make sure the fire got real hot—hot enough to take the round yard up with it.'

Nick squatted on his haunches, poking around in the charred remains. She saw him glance across at something lying on the ground to one side, saw him reach out to pick it up.

'What is it?' she asked from behind.

Nick peered at the object in his hand. 'It's nothing,' he said, his fingers closing over it. Kate felt a protest catch in her throat. In the second before it vanished from sight, she had identified the small object. A matchbox!

She felt the ground tilt as the implication of the find hit her. A serious discovery like that...evidence, perhaps...and Nick had chosen to hide it from her! *Why*?

'The fire's out, Nick!' Joe called out, dragging the fire hose away, the air around them heavy with the smell of ashes and charred timber.

'OK, let's mop up and go home,' said Nick, rising. 'There's not much more we can do now. I'll come back at first light and take a closer look around. We'll be lucky to find any tracks or footprints with all these hoofmarks around, and our own scuffmarks, but you never know.'

'I'll come with you,' Kate said at once, and flushed, hoping it didn't sound as if she wanted to check up on him. Oh, Nick, she thought with a renewed rush of shame, I know you didn't start this fire...you were with me all evening. And I can't, I *won't* believe you would have asked anybody else to do a thing like this. But, Nick, you're hiding *something*.

As she followed Smithy back to the water truck she turned, her eyes seeking Nick's, clinging to them briefly in the darkness. Nobody, she tried to tell him with her eyes, will be happier than I'll be, Nick, if we do find some tracks in the morning, tracks that lead us to the real culprit. Because, Nick, I simply couldn't bear it if it does turn out that you're in some way responsible for all this. No matter how justified you might feel after the terrible wrong that was done to you in the past, and no matter how badly you want Ramsay Downs...I simply couldn't bear it!

* * *

She hardly slept a wink that night. The only explanation she could come up with for Nick wanting to hide evidence from her was that he knew who had dropped the matchbox there and for reasons of his own he didn't want *her* to know. Which seemed to suggest that Nick must have sent the person there himself, that he was working hand in glove with him.

Or with her.

She held her breath. Abigail?

Her heart plunged to her toes. Were the two of them in this together after all? Had they joined forces to try to drive her out, because they both wanted Ramsay Downs... and each other?

'Oh, Nick...' An almost unbearable pain twisted inside her, and she whispered into the darkness, 'Just when I was beginning to trust you! Just when I was beginning to hope that you might even... care a little.'

She gave a derisive snort. What kind of fool did that make her? Just because he'd shown her a little kindness... just because he'd held her in his arms a couple of times, simply *to comfort her* ... It might have done all kinds of things to her, but it didn't mean he had been affected in any way at all!

Jeremy's handsome face swam in front of her, his blue eyes taunting her. 'It's time you faced reality, Kate... Do you honestly believe that my saintly half-brother would ever fall for a woman who used to be married to me? After what I did to him? If you believe that, then you're living in fantasy land!'

A tear glistened on the tip of Kate's eyelashes. Resolutely she thought of the matchbox Nick had hidden from her, and a slow anger started simmering inside her, gradually mounting, stifling her misery, stifling any lingering, foolish fantasies.

*   *   *

The morning air was frosty, the sky streaked with wisps of pink and purple when Kate, her eyes deeply shadowed after her restless night, met Nick in the yard.

By now she was in just the mood to face him—and she was going to let nothing, nothing, stop her having her say.

'I feel it's only fair to let you know, Nick,' she said, facing him with sparks in her eyes, 'that nothing is going to make me leave Ramsay Downs. No matter what else happens, I won't be running away. I'm not leaving... ever. So if—if that's the only reason you're staying on here, you might as well go now.'

A crackling silence filled the crisp morning air. She saw a tiny yellow flame flicker in Nick's black eyes, but she wasn't sure what it meant. She bit back a gasp as he took a step closer and slipped his hand round her waist, pulling her towards him.

'D-don't, Nick!' With a violent jerk she twisted free and pulled back out of his reach. She couldn't think straight when he touched her. 'That won't make me change my mind—nothing will!'

Instead of reacting angrily, he looked amused, if anything, holding up his hands as if to show her he wasn't about to pounce on her. 'Kate, it's all right. I'm not trying to make you change your mind. I don't want you to go.'

She stared at him. 'You d-don't? But—but you've said all along——'

'Yes, well, that was before.'

'Before?' Something clenched in her stomach. A crazy, illogical hope.

As he paused, as if weighing something in his mind, she had a flash of insight. 'Before I found out about

Jeremy?' she breathed. '*That's* why you wanted me to go? So I wouldn't find out?'

He spread his hands. 'I was hoping you'd never have to know, Kate. It was something between him and me, nothing to do with you. Kate, don't let it spoil what you shared with Jeremy. I'm sorry you had to find out. I never wanted that.'

She gulped. 'That was considerate of you, Nick.' She drew in a fluttery breath. Something was still puzzling her. 'But, Nick, you always said that *you* wanted Ramsay Downs...that you wanted to put down roots here.'

With Abigail? she pondered bleakly.

'Kate...in the beginning I didn't expect that you'd *want* to stay. I thought you were only staying on here because you felt that you owed it to Jeremy. You talked about carrying out his dream...'

She flushed. 'I thought Jeremy loved Ramsay Downs, that it meant everything to him. But now I'm not so sure. I think he was more obsessed with not wanting *you* to have it.' She hesitated, biting her lip. 'Nick, do you still want it? It *is* your old home. Are you...disappointed that I've decided to stay on here?' She looked searchingly into his eyes.

His gaze didn't waver. 'I can live without Ramsay Downs, Kate.' He paused to let that sink in, then said, 'It belongs to you. I can see now that you belong to it too. I can see how much you've come to love this place.'

She gulped back a wave of emotion. 'But, Nick, only yesterday you were still saying you wanted me to leave...'

'I was worried about your safety.'

'And you're not now?' She felt a swift pang.

'Kate, I have a hunch who's been doing all these things. I've had an uneasy suspicion all along...'

Her heart missed a beat. 'Who?' she whispered.

He seemed to hesitate. Then, 'I need to be very sure first. Trust me, Kate. You do trust me now, don't you?' he asked, his gaze holding hers.

She clasped her hands to her chest, hardly breathing, a tangle of emotions warring inside her, emotions she had been fighting from the first moment she had met him. Whether she trusted him or not suddenly didn't seem the all-important thing any more.

Nick, I love you, she realised, the truth hitting her like a thunderbolt for the first time. I love you with all my heart, and that's all that matters!

She stared up at him, stunned at the realisation. She loved Nick as she had never loved any man before. What she had felt for Jeremy... it had been nothing like this. It had been a shallow, lukewarm emotion, a girlish infatuation compared to what she felt now for Nick. She loved him so much, wanted him so much, that she knew now that she would forgive him anything, overlook anything he had done, if only he would stay, if only he would come to love her too, in time.

She reached out tentatively and touched his arm. 'I—I do trust you, Nick, I *do*, but...' Her eyes appealed to him. 'Won't you... confide in me? I—I saw you pick up a matchbox last night. A matchbox, Nick! It could be evidence—and yet you've kept it from me. *Why*?'

'Ah,' he nodded slowly, 'so that's it!' He sighed heavily. 'I don't think it means anything, Kate, that's why I didn't say anything.'

'What do you mean—doesn't mean anything? A *matchbox*, Nick?' She shook her head. 'I don't...'

'I think it was planted there.'

'Planted?' Her brow puckered. 'Why would...? Nick, show it to me. I want to see it!'

'Well, don't go jumping to any conclusions,' Nick dug resignedly into his pocket and handed her a small gold packet.

She took it from him. 'It's...a matchbox from Helsinki,' she said, frowning. '"The Marski Hotel, Helsinki",' she read aloud. Her head jerked up. The only person she knew of who collected foreign matchboxes was—— 'Danny!' she burst out. Her eyes clouded in confusion. 'But—but Danny was in town last night, with James.'

'Precisely.'

'Unless—unless he left James and...' She let the rest trail off with a groan. 'Oh, Nick, I can't believe that Danny would...but if he...how else...?'

'You see?' Nick mocked gently. 'Already you're starting to believe it. Because of this!' He prodded the matchbox with an angry finger.

'And you...don't?' Bewildered, she looked up at him.

'No, I don't. I've had experience, remember, of evidence being planted. So too has Minya.'

Kate's hand fluttered to her throat. Jeremy again! 'And—and now you think——'

'I think somebody else could be using the same tactics, planting evidence to shift suspicion and point the finger at...Danny. Luckily for Danny, the past has taught me not to accept things at face value.'

'Oh, Nick, you're right. How brilliant!' Kate felt a wave of relief, but it was mingled with shame. How could she ever have believed that Nick would be involved in anything underhand...that he and Abigail could have...?

She let her eyelids flutter down, a shaft of pain stabbing through her at the thought of Abigail. Even if Nick had accepted the fact that she, Kate, was staying on here at Ramsay Downs, he might well still want

Abigail. Maybe, now that he knew where he stood, he would decide to buy another property elsewhere . . . with Abigail. Hadn't she seen him whispering sweet nothings in Abigail's all-too-willing ear at Doon-gara the other day? Did he . . . love her?

She swallowed hard, and pushed the painful thought aside.

'If this was just a plant,' she said slowly, holding up the matchbox, 'how do you intend to find the real culprit? You said you had some idea who it might be . . . But how can you, Nick? You haven't even looked for tracks yet!'

'Call it a sixth sense. I'd like you to leave it to me, Kate. When is Danny due back?'

'Some time this morning. You think he might be able to help?'

'Maybe. If he can remember giving the matchbox to someone—or remember someone not handing it back to him. Send him out to the drafting yards, will you, when he gets back? We'll all be out there. I want the men to start clearing up, ready to rebuild. In the meantime . . .'

'Yes?' She glanced up at him. Had his eyes softened, or was that just wishful thinking?

'If you have any urgent jobs that need doing, get them done today.' He trailed his fingers along her arm, causing her nerve ends to tingle in response. 'Tomorrow we're going up north.'

'Up north?' She took a quick sharp breath. 'You mean——'

He nodded. 'I think it's time you knew exactly what was on your own land, Kate.'

Kate's tongue flicked over her lips. 'I'd like that, Nick,' she said, aware that her heart was thudding slowly in her chest. 'You...don't want me to come out to the yards with you?'

'No need ... you catch up on whatever needs doing here. I'll take the motorbike out.' Nick reached out to touch her cheek, and his palm was like fire on her skin. It was all she could do to stop herself seizing his hand and pressing it to her lips. 'Keep your radio open in case we need each other.'

Need each other? Nick, I'll always need you, she tried to tell him with her eyes. But will you ever need me? She turned away before her eyes told him any more, before they told him too much.

She spent the day catching up on a backlog of paperwork and doing odd jobs around the homestead, but her mind never left Nick for a second. Was he still out at the drafting yards, she wondered, or had he gone off somewhere by now, following some trail? His radio had been silent since mid-morning, when she had let him know that Danny and James were on their way out there.

She stood on the veranda, staring yearningly across the deserted yard. Nick seemed confident that he was on the right track. If anyone could find the culprit, it would be Nick. She had the utmost faith in his capabilities.

But...a cold knot formed in her stomach...what then? Once he had unmasked whoever it was and the danger was behind them, would he then decide that it was time to leave?

She clasped her hands together and pressed them to her lips. If she asked him to stay on would he? If she offered to make him a partner? They made a good team...there was no doubt about that. And maybe, just maybe, in time...

She turned away with a sigh. There was still Abigail. And even if Abigail wasn't involved with Nick, there was still the spectre of Jeremy, and what he had done to Nick in the past. She might be able to close her mind to all that...but could Nick? Wouldn't Jeremy always be there between them?

To Nick he would be.

She was living in fantasy land again.

She snatched up the two-way radio when she heard Nick's voice.

'Yes, Nick, I'm here. Over.'

'Hi. Everything all right? Over.' His voice was gentle, like a caress.

'Yes, fine. Where are you? Still out at the yards? Over.'

'No, I left some time ago. Look, I won't be back in time for dinner. Don't wait for me.'

Kate's heart dipped. 'Where are you?' Was he still looking for tracks? 'Can't I bring something out to you? Food? Drinks? Over.'

'No need—I've eaten. The boys made a campfire earlier and cooked some snags and boiled a billy. Kate, there's something I have to do. I may be late back. I want you to get a good night's sleep—we'll need to leave early in the morning, around six. Ask Minya to pack some lunch for us, will you? Take care, Kate.'

The radio went dead.

Kate sank into a chair. Why wouldn't he tell her where he was going? Was he on the trail of...?

She clenched her hands into fists, her heart seizing up in her chest. Was it likely to be *dangerous*?

Oh, Nick, why won't you tell me who it is you suspect? Is it one of my own men? Is that why you're being so cautious? Because you want to be quite sure before you say anything to me?

She clung to anger to hide the anxiety she felt. 'Damn you, Nick Ramsay, we're supposed to be pulling together, working as a team! A fine partner you'd make! You might have confided in me, taken me with you!'

She jumped up and started pacing round, unable to settle to anything after that. As the shadows lengthened and the sky gradually turned from blue to pink to vivid orange, she heard the sound of Danny's ute in the yard. She flew outside.

'Danny! James! At last!' She ran to meet them as they clambered out of the ute, soot-streaked and weary. 'Do you know where Nick's gone?' she asked breathlessly.

'Nick?' James shook his head. 'He didn't actually say. But the last we saw of him he was heading south, towards Doon-gara.'

Doon-gara! Kate caught her breath. To see...Abigail? She felt a swift stab of jealousy.

'We'd better go in and clean up,' Danny put in. Was he avoiding her eye?

She glared after them as Danny hustled James into the house. Danny, she thought, knows more than he's saying.

She felt a surge of annoyance at being kept in the dark. Why all the secrecy?

Nick was heading towards Doon-gara, James had said. If not to see Abigail, then . . .

Surely it couldn't mean that Nick suspected someone at Doon-gara? Kate bit her lip and frowned. If he did, why would he feel the need to keep his suspicions from *her*?

Because it was someone he knew . . . an old friend, perhaps?

She caught her breath as another more shocking thought followed. Surely Nick couldn't suspect Abigail herself! Abigail...working on her own? Could that be why he was being so secretive?

She slumped against the wooden veranda post. Abigail had been here the night the mare was set free...and she lived within easy reach of Ramsay Downs! It wouldn't be beyond a woman to poison a water trough, to pour sand and cement into a windmill, to start a fire...leaving a matchbox of Danny's lying around to incriminate him, unaware that he had gone into town last night with James. The girl could have pocketed that matchbox of Danny's any time. Maybe during her brother's engagement party.

Kate gripped the veranda post for support. Could it possibly be true? Abigail had made no secret of the fact that she wanted Kate to go, that she had her sights set on Nick...

But if Nick truly did suspect Abigail, why would he keep his suspicions to himself? Because he loved her? Kate's fingernails dug into the rounded timber. Had he gone to Doon-gara to warn Abigail to be careful...to tell her that she had gone too far, and that she should stop before she was caught? Maybe right this minute, in the belief that Ramsay Downs was slipping out of his reach, Nick was pleading with Abigail to go away with him and find another property elsewhere!

Kate moaned, a sick despair sweeping over her.

Desperation gave her the strength to rally, to fight. There was still tomorrow. Tomorrow Nick had promised to take her up north. She would have him to herself, all day...

She dragged herself slowly up the steps. Whatever was up there—gold, minerals, whatever—Nick could have it all. Would that make him stay? She would offer him a partnership as well. She was prepared to fight for him. Maybe he wasn't completely committed to Abigail...yet.

Oh, Nick, she thought, I love you so much...and I won't let you go, I *won't*!

CHAPTER TEN

DESPITE yet another disturbed night, she was up at the crack of dawn, ready to meet Nick on the dot of six, as arranged.

'Good morning,' he said breezily, and Kate's heart rolled over at the sight of him, his hair still damp from his early morning shower, his step jaunty, his eyes a bright glitter under the heavy brows. He looked as if he at least had had a good night's sleep. She had heard the whine of his motorbike around midnight, as she was restlessly tossing in her bed, so she knew he hadn't stayed at Doon-gara all night. A small consolation, she reflected wryly.

He looked wonderful—or was it that she was simply seeing him with new eyes? He was wearing much the same as he normally wore—a bushman's shirt, tight moleskins, leather belt, elastic-sided boots, but she was conscious, as never before, of the way he wore them, of the way his shirt was stretched across his chest, showing the taut muscles underneath, the way his leather belt sat low on his hips, above the strong thighs, the way the rising sun struck his tanned face, accentuating the strong bones and square jaw. She found her eyes tracing the deep cleft in his chin, the sensuous curve of his mouth, as if she had never noticed them properly before.

'You look a little tired, Kate,' he said, his voice a low rumble, and she gave a faint start, realising he must have been scrutinising her as closely as she had him. 'Everything all right?'

She summoned a smile, the most dazzling smile she could muster. She wanted to enjoy this day, and she wanted Nick to enjoy it too—with her. 'Just fine. I'm looking forward to our trip.' Realising he must think it a bit odd that she hadn't asked him about what he had been doing yesterday, she broached it tentatively. 'Did you have any luck yesterday?'

'We can talk about that later. I want to make a start, so that we're up there by lunchtime. Pop the icebox in the back. Couldn't be a better day, could it, for a picnic lunch?'

Kate gave him an oblique look. He was as good as telling her that he wanted her to contain her curiosity until they were well away from the homestead. Why? To make sure they could talk freely, without interruption? Or—she felt her heart sink—did he simply want to put off telling her for as long as he could?

She pushed her qualms aside and gave him another brilliant smile. She wasn't even going to think about it! She was going to enjoy her day with Nick... enjoy it for as long as she could, at any rate. It just might be the last time.

The jeep reared and plunged over the uneven ground as they finally left the graded road and struck north-west through an area of uncleared brigalow, where the track was barely visible in the thick undergrowth. A flock of galahs, shrieking their displeasure, fluttered into the air at their approach, a spectacular explosion of brilliant colour, soaring overhead in a wash of pink that magically turned to grey. Two furry grey kangaroos were startled out of their placid grazing and bounded off into the distance in long graceful leaps.

Despite the jolts, Kate was still smiling, feeling relaxed and happy after almost three hours of driving, revelling in Nick's company. The sky overhead was a brilliant blue and the late May sun blazed down, more like summer than late autumn. Twice on the long drive north Nick had pulled out the canvas water bag to offer her a refreshing drink.

On the way they had had plenty of distractions to keep their minds occupied, seizing the chance to check dams and fences, to spy out cattle to see which ones were in prime condition and which ones were falling off for some reason, to note which paddocks had enough feed and how long they were likely to support cattle, and to share some spectacular sights: the sharp purple peaks of a distant mountain range, stark against the clear blue sky; a glint of blue through the trees from a tranquil billabong; the shadowy white trunk of a ghost gum caught in the rays of the sun, its branches twisted into grotesque shapes.

'Oh, look, Nick!' Kate cried as she spotted an emu in deep grass that reached almost to its chest. As they drove past, it began rushing from side to side in a frantic fashion.

'What's she doing?' she asked, watching captivated, as the emu pranced about like an undersized ostrich.

Nick laughed. 'I'd say she has chicks...and she's worried about them. OK, OK, old girl,' he shouted through the open window, 'we're just passing by. No need to have a heart attack!'

As they bounced into wilder, more rugged country, they had glimpses, every now and again, of great ridges of granite rock, standing out like fiery beacons in the rays of the sun, spinifex and roly-poly clinging tenaciously to the rock-face.

This was new territory to Kate, inaccessible to cattle, and she felt her pulse quicken.

'Hold on to your hat!' yelled Nick, easing the vehicle into a lower gear and edging it slowly through a shallow rock-strewn watercourse and up on to the opposite bank.

'Are we nearly there?' Kate asked breathlessly, and he nodded.

'Not far now,' he said, and something in his voice made her sense that he was as excited as she.

They entered a deep gorge through a rift in the cliffs, and after a neck-jerking ride along a dry rocky creek bed, Nick slewed the vehicle round and parked it in the shade of a rock wall, surprising four emus, which fled away through the quivering bushes like old ladies in bustles.

As Kate sat for a moment catching her breath, Nick handed her the water-bag. She gulped the cold water with the eagerness of someone staggering out of the desert after days without water. 'Now...' His lips stretched into a smile, his warm hand briefly brushing hers. 'Want to get out and stretch your legs?'

She swallowed, feeling suddenly nervous—whether it was his smile, his touch, or the excitement of the moment, she couldn't have said. She nodded, giving a shaky smile in return before throwing open her door.

The pungent scent of eucalypts hit her as she stepped out. There was a sunny midday hush; not a breath of wind, the stillness filled with the shrilling of cicadas.

'Aah!' She threw out her chest and stretched her arms, gulping in deep breaths of fresh air.

'That better?'

At the sound of Nick's voice she turned. 'Oh, look, Nick!' she cried, delighted. The delicate head of a small rock wallaby was peeping at her from behind a cluster of boulders above his shoulder. As Nick moved the small animal bounded off in a flash of brown and grey, the ancient camouflage for survival.

'Is—is this where Jeremy came?' she asked in a hushed voice, remembering the real reason they had come here. When he nodded, his eyes hardening momentarily, she turned away, her gaze flickering along the dry bed of the gorge, a tumble of stones and boulders lying along its length. Jeremy had said he had stumbled on the gold nugget in a remote rocky creek bed. This must be the place where he had found it.

And where Logan Ramsay's father had been killed by the Aborigines.

Kate shivered. There was something about this place, an atmosphere, that made her feel uneasy.

'Nick, why do you want this land?' she burst out. 'You say you don't want the gold—assuming there *is* gold here.'

'Didn't Jeremy prove that there is?' said Nick, his voice harsh in the stillness. 'No, I don't want the gold. Do *you*?' he asked, his eyes boring into hers.

'N-not if you want the land, Nick.'

He made an impatient sound. 'The only reason I want this land, Kate, is to stop anyone else getting their hands on it. More specifically, to stop anyone digging into this hill for gold. Or for any other reason.'

'Ah,' she said, beginning to understand. 'You want it to remain untouched.' She glanced up at the rugged red cliffs, with their deep fissures and moss-covered overhangs of rock. Snowy white ghost gums clung to crevices in the rock wall. 'I can understand that. It's very beautiful here. A bit remote, though, don't you think? A bit...spooky, too, in a way.'

Nick's face eased into a lop-sided smile. 'Maybe there's a reason for that.'

She looked faintly startled. 'What do you mean? Are there still Aborigines around here?'

'Come with me.' He held out his hand, and when he had hers firmly clasped in his he began pulling her up the rocky slope, clambering over a tumble of boulders at its base.

A rainbow bird flashed overhead, and she jumped in fright.

Nick's hand tightened on hers. 'It's not far up,' he said. They climbed higher, following a deep fissure in the rock. Then he stopped, and stood back. 'There!'

On one side of the fissure was the entrance to a cave, half screened by rocks and bushes.

'You'd never know it was here!' Kate said in a whisper.

They climbed a few more paces and went in. The cave opened into a much larger cave, extending from it along the cliff face.

Kate gazed around in awe. She found she was standing in a huge gallery of Aboriginal cave paintings.

There were drawings everywhere, of weapons, snakes, crocodiles, horses, kangaroos, human fertility figures— rows and rows of faded paintings and blurred engravings stretching around the walls and roof, and continuing into an adjoining gallery.

'So this is what you want to protect,' she breathed, understanding at last. 'It's a treasure-house!'

'They've been here for thousands of years,' said Nick, close behind her. 'The family have always known they were here... but we've told few people about them. We didn't want strangers coming here, desecrating them.'

Kate turned slowly to face him. Instead, his own brother had threatened to destroy the caves, by digging into the hill for gold. 'Now I understand why Jeremy swore me to secrecy about the gold,' she said heavily. 'It wasn't to stop you demanding a share or to stop you trying to take the gold or the land from him—he was afraid you might find out what he had in mind and stop *him* getting his hands on the gold. Nick, I'm so ashamed.'

He reached out to clasp her arm. 'Kate, you can't blame yourself. Why do you think he never told you about these caves? Because he knew you'd feel the same way I do about disturbing them, destroying them.'

She bit her lip. 'That's very generous of you, Nick,' she said huskily. She blinked and turned away. Why ever had it taken her so long to see the goodness in Nick? Or had she seen it all along, and merely closed her mind to it, swayed as she had been by Jeremy's lies? And now... was it too late? Had she lost him... to Abigail?

She shook the painful thought away. She wasn't going to let anything spoil this day. 'Didn't you say your grandfather was born here, Nick?' she asked, remembering what he had once told her.

'Not here in these caves, but in one nearby,' Nick said, moving in close behind her. 'Even the Aborigines stay away from this place. This is a sorcery site, and they're very superstitious. They say it was evil spirits that killed Logan's father when he came here.'

'I can believe it,' Kate said with a shiver.

She felt his hands slip over her shoulders. 'It wasn't, of course. Some Aborigines followed him here, and they killed him. They were afraid he was going to desecrate their sacred site when he started digging for gold.'

'Do you think Jeremy would have been in danger too, if he'd come back here and tried to do the same?' Kate asked in a low voice, thinking with a gulp that it would have been only what he deserved.

'What happened to Logan's father happened a long time ago, Kate,' said Nick, his fingers gently kneading her shoulders from behind. 'The thing is, no one *is* going to dig this place up. I'm going to make sure of that.'

She twisted round to face him. 'You don't need to worry, Nick. Now that I know what's here, I'd never let it happen either. Not that it will be up to me. I still want you to have this land, Nick. It belongs to you.'

'Let's get out of here,' Nick said quietly, and as they moved away, he advised, 'Walk where I walk. They didn't paint snakes here for nothing.'

'Oh, lovely!' She was glad when they emerged into the bright sunlight. 'Er—where were you planning to have lunch?' she asked tentatively as they clambered down the rocky slope. 'At a safe distance from the evil spirits, I trust?'

'Well away,' he assured her with a smile that softened his features and brought a warm glow to his eyes—at the same time melting all her defences. 'I know just the spot.'

It was only a five-minute drive away, in a nearby gully, where Nick spread out a groundsheet on a wide rocky ledge, in the shade of a clump of stringybarks. Secret places in the rocks had cupped fresh water from recent rains, and they scooped some up in their hands and splashed it over their faces.

'And now lunch,' said Kate, rubbing her hands, realising suddenly that she was hungry. As she stepped over to where she had left the lunch basket she heard a rustling sound in the grass and saw a grey scaly head poke out from a clump of rocks. She gave a squeal and spun round, her feet slipping on some loose stones and flying from underneath her. Nick caught her as she toppled over, lost his own balance, and together they landed in a tangle of arms and legs on the groundsheet, with Kate sprawled across him.

'Oh!' she gasped. 'Sorry, Nick. Are you all right?' She wriggled until she was lying stretched out beside him, though she made sure she didn't wriggle out of his arms as well, leaning in close, nestling comfortably against him.

'Never better.' Grinning down at her, he brought a hand up to cup her chin. 'It was only a lizard—a blue-tongue. Quite harmless.'

She giggled. 'I thought it was a snake!' She looked up into his eyes, and his black gaze seemed to swallow her. They both grew still, the laughter dying on their lips. For an endless moment they lay staring at each other, the air heavy and silent around them, even the cicadas falling silent.

And then with a muffled groan Nick lowered his head and brought his mouth down on hers, devouring her lips hungrily, his hand moving over her shoulderblades, exploring the hollows of her back as he crushed her against the full length of his body. She felt a hot intense flame lick upward from somewhere deep within her, and she drank in his kiss, her lips softening, parting beneath his, her fingers clutching at his chest as she returned his kiss with reckless abandon.

She felt his hand raking through the honeyed mass of her hair, and with an inarticulate little cry she brought her arms up and curled them round his neck, her hands trembling with passion.

Her lips clung to his, his kiss arousing her to wild heights of urgent passion, her senses reeling in wonder. How could a mere kiss be so devastating, so totally, earth-shatteringly different from every other kiss she had ever known, even the intimate kisses she had at one time shared with her own husband? Nick made her feel as if she had never really been kissed before. He was arousing in her a depth of passion she had never experienced before, urgent needs that had long been unrealised, that were clamouring to be explored and satisfied.

'Kate...' Her name came thickly from his throat as he dragged his mouth away from hers and covered her face and neck with kiss after kiss, his lips fiery on her skin. She felt her heart crashing inside her chest, her lungs snatching at air as if she had no breath left.

As his lips claimed hers again, she pressed her body feverishly against him, her breasts rubbing against the warm strength of his chest, drawing a deep groan from him. She felt urgent fingers tugging at her blouse, felt his hand glide up her bare midriff to cover the soft swell of her breast, his fingers stroking the smooth flesh above the thin lacy covering.

She made sounds of anguished pleasure as he slipped his fingers underneath the lace and squeezed the sensitive swollen peak with his thumb and forefinger, sending exquisite needles of pleasure shooting through her. She arched her body against him, wanting him with a wild need that made her whole body shudder and burn.

He muttered something against her lips. 'Nick?' she murmured languorously, her voice muffled under the hungry motion of his mouth. Breathing heavily, he drew back his head and looked into her eyes, the black glitter of his gaze turning her bones to heavy, molten treacle. 'Kate, you're driving me insane...'

'Nick,' she said weakly, almost crying out her love for him. But she managed to catch the words back in time, her dazed eyes gradually focusing on his face as she dragged herself back to reality with an effort. With a shuddering sigh she gently pushed the hand on her breast aside and reluctantly rolled back away from him and sat up. She couldn't let this go on. She could tell by the tension in him, by the harsh unevenness of his breathing, that Nick was fast losing control, and she knew that if he did she wouldn't have the strength to deny him, to deny her own burning needs; it was hard enough to turn him away now.

But he didn't love her—he had never said he loved her, and much as she loved him she would be foolish to give in to him, to let her own feelings sweep her away, when there was still so much unresolved between them: Abigail, the spectre of Jeremy, Nick's long-term plans...far too many things. When—if—Nick ever made love to her, fully and completely, she wanted it to be right... perfect...for both of them.

'Nick, I——'

He stopped the rest with a kiss, no more than a light brush of his lips this time. 'Lunch,' he said, his tone faintly rueful. 'If we don't have it soon, the ants and the flies will.' He waved her back as she made a move to get up. 'Allow me... I'll fetch the icebox this time.'

They unpacked it in the shade of the trees, realising, as they began to eat, how ravenous they were. Kate had prepared the lunch herself—crusty bread rolls, chunks of cold beef and cheese, hard-boiled eggs, firm ripe tomatoes, some of Minya's sultana cake, and some fresh fruit. They ate every morsel. When Nick offered her a cool drink afterwards, she took a deep nervous breath and said, 'Nick, I don't want you to leave Ramsay Downs.'

'Oh?' he said, raising a thick eyebrow and leaning lazily back against a moss-covered rock. 'Care to elaborate on that?'

Her hands twisted nervously in her lap. He wasn't going to make this easy for her! 'Nick, I need you,' she said simply. 'I can't manage without you.' What I mean, Nick, she added silently, in desperation, is... I can't *live* without you! She closed her mind resolutely to thoughts of Abigail. Maybe, with enough enticement, she could make him forget Abigail.

'There are plenty of good overseers around,' Nick drawled. His black eyes, mere slits against the harsh rays of sunlight piercing the branches, were giving nothing away. 'They're not all like Leif Clancy.'

Kate felt a swift wave of panic. He couldn't be considering leaving! Not *now*. Hadn't that kiss meant anything to him? She pressed her hands to her chest in sudden doubt. Just because it had moved the earth for her it didn't mean it had affected him in the same way. He could have been merely carried away by the heat of the moment. For all she knew he might still want to move away and settle down somewhere else with...Abigail. She couldn't let that happen!

'Nick, I don't mean——' She broke off impatiently and came straight to the point. 'I mean I want you to stay on as—as part-owner, Nick...to have a half-share of Ramsay Downs. You—you once suggested a partnership, remember?' Of course, he hadn't expected her to stay on then. He had wanted sole control, imagining she would be well out of his way, back home in Sydney where she belonged, a silent partner with no real part to play. But now that he knew she intended to stay on here for good, would he feel differently about accepting a partnership? And where would Abigail fit in if he did accept?

'Mmm...yes, I do recall.' Nick tapped his chin with a finger, as if giving the idea his earnest consideration. 'A partnership, eh? Well, now, I wonder...'

Kate's chest felt as if it would burst with tension. What was holding him back? Was he thinking of Abigail?

Abigail, Abigail! Her eyes flashed with sudden purpose. She had to know what Abigail meant to him. This uncertainty was driving her crazy!

'Nick, is Abigail the reason you're thinking of leaving?' The question burst out.

'Abigail?' She saw genuine surprise in his eyes. 'What in the world makes you think that?'

She gulped. 'Well, *you* did,' she accused. 'The way you—you...' Her hand fluttered helplessly in the air. 'And the way she...' Realising she was making no sense, she broke off crossly. Damn, damn, damn, she thought. Why did I stupidly have to bring Abigail's name into this? She abruptly changed tack.

'Nick, never mind any of that now. Look, about yesterday... you've kept me in suspense quite long enough.
Are you going to tell me what happened or not?'

'You mean I haven't told you?' he said teasingly, and
she grabbed a stick and threw it at him. 'OK, OK, I
surrender!' Sobering, he said, 'You've nothing more to
worry about, Kate, on that score. I uncovered our culprit.
And it's all over. Finished. Nothing else is going to
happen.'

Kate stopped breathing for a second. 'How—how can
you be so sure?' she whispered finally. The question she
most wanted to ask—*who*?—seemed to have stuck in
her throat. 'You mean you've confronted him—and he's
confessed?'

'Not him, Kate. *Her*.'

Her! 'You mean it *was* Abigail?'

'You suspected it was her?' Surprise flared in his eyes.

She shrugged, and bowed her head, her soft hair falling
across her face. 'James mentioned that you were heading
south yesterday, towards Doon-gara,' she explained. 'I
just... had a feeling.' But feelings and reality were two
very different things. It still came as a shock. She wasn't
sure how she felt. Numbed, if anything. 'And she...she's
never made any secret of the fact that she wants me to
leave,' she added in a flat voice. 'Nick...' her head jerked
up again 'why didn't you tell me you suspected her?'
she asked with difficulty. She found she was holding her
breath.

'I had to be sure, Kate. I had no real proof... just a
gut feeling and some tyre marks belonging to a Doon-
gara vehicle that anybody could have been driving. And
a matchbox that Danny couldn't recall Abigail handing
back to him at the barbecue. I had to tread carefully. I

thought she was more likely to confess to me than to... anyone else.'

'Than me, you mean,' said Kate, and sighed. 'And she did? She actually confessed?'

Nick's mouth twisted. 'Oh, yes, and she was proud of it too. She seemed to think she was doing me a good turn.' He rolled over beside her, his hand closing gently on her arm. 'Kate, in the end I decided not to take any formal action against her. And I hope you'll agree with me.'

Kate looked at him for a long moment, feeling a heaviness, like a lead weight, pressing down on her. He must still care about her, then. 'You don't want her getting into any trouble over it?'

'Kate, it's not that. We thrashed it all out, and in the end she—well, she convinced me it was for the best. The important thing is, Kate, you'll have no more worries—it's over. Abigail pleaded with me to keep quiet about it, to let it drop—not only for her own sake, but to spare her family. I agreed, on one condition.'

Kate summoned up enough strength to ask faintly, 'What condition?'

'That she go away. And now, Kate, she's gone.'

'Gone? Gone where?' Kate whispered, pain clutching at her heart. Gone somewhere to wait for him?

'She's gone back to her husband.'

Kate's eyes snapped wide. 'But—but she hates her husband! She told me he's a monster, a tyrant.'

Nick gave a harsh laugh. 'Only because he refused to give in to her and let her have her own way the whole time. The trouble with Abigail is, she's been spoilt. She's always demanded, never given. But I'd say she's finally met her match in her second husband. Bevan, it appears, won't stand for her tantrums. Why do you think she walked out on him? Because he put his foot down about something and she couldn't take it. She stormed out and came running back home, expecting him to come chasing after her. When he didn't, she thought her marriage was over, finished. She tried to convince herself she didn't care by chasing after me.'

Kate swallowed. 'You didn't seem to mind being chased!'

'Mm... not jealous, were you, Kate?'

'Certainly not!' She gave him a sharp look. 'You don't mean you were trying to *make* me jealous?'

She saw his chest heave and fall. 'No, Kate, it wasn't that. It was more a case of trying to hide what I was feeling for you. Because I could see no future in it—not with you believing what Jeremy had told you about me. And I certainly wasn't going to be the one to disillusion you. I never wanted that to happen, Kate. I hoped it never would.'

Kate was glad she was sitting down. Her head was spinning. '*Trying to hide what I was feeling for you,*' he had said. She gulped, and admitted with a sigh, 'I think in a lot of ways I was already disillusioned, Nick. Jeremy was never the same after he realised we weren't going to have a child. He threw himself back into his polo and we... grew apart. It hurt me, but at the time I blamed myself, for not giving him the son he wanted. Then when he died I realised he must have turned away from me because he was worried about... failing me somehow, being inadequate. I felt so guilty... for not being more perceptive, for not showing more understanding.'

'Kate, you can't blame yourself. You weren't to know... and Jeremy would have hated it if you had. He never had any patience with sickness...he wouldn't have wanted your sympathy.'

Her lashes swept down, shadowing her eyes. 'I didn't know him very well at all, I realise now. He never confided in me, or took the time to really get to know me.' She sighed, and glanced up, meeting Nick steadily in the eye. 'So you see, Nick, we were never as close as you thought,' she said heavily. 'Those last months of our marriage, he completely shut me out. Even before then, what we did share didn't go very deep, I'm afraid, not even when we...' She flushed, and let the rest trail off.

'But he did love you, Kate,' Nick said gently. 'It was apparent to everyone who saw you together...Minya, the Stantons, the stockmen who were here at the time...'

'Maybe he did love me, in his own way,' she conceded with a sigh. He had loved her, she guessed, as much as he was capable of loving anyone. Certainly he had never looked at another woman in all the time she had known him. 'But how can I ever forgive him, Nick, for what he did to you?' she cried. 'The hurt you must have suffered...the danger...being sent away...everything.'

'Kate...' pulling her against him, Nick folded her in his arms '...when you think of Jeremy, try to remember him as he was when he married you, when you were happy together...don't dwell on what he did to me.'

She looked up at him, her eyes misting, shimmering green pools under glistening lashes. 'It's no wonder your family loved you so much, Nick.'

'There's only one person's love I want now.' His eyes held hers, the black depths smouldering with a tenderness that stopped the breath in her throat.

'Nick, are you saying...?'

'I'm saying I love you, Kate, more than I ever thought it possible to love a woman.' He trailed his hand up her bare arm and let it rest on the silky curve of her throat, sending a wave of liquid heat through her limbs. 'I'd almost given up hope of finding a woman like you, Kate—a woman I would love so much I'd want to spend the rest of my life in one place, with one woman. Before I met you, marriage was never high on my agenda...I've always been on the move so much.' He shifted so that her head nestled comfortably into the curve of his shoulder. 'And then, in the ultimate irony, when I did find the special woman I'd been looking for, she was my brother's widow...and she despised me.'

'No, Nick!' Kate twisted in his arms, her eyes leaping to his in instant denial. She was having difficulty breathing, with his hand now moving sensuously over the sensitive swell of her breast. 'I never despised *you*...that was the whole trouble. I despised what I believed you'd done to your brother. But...oh, Nick, that first time you kissed me...' She felt her cheeks flame at the memory. 'And then you pushed me away and I—I felt so humiliated and confused...'

He dropped a light kiss on her brow. 'Whatever I might have said at the time, Kate, the truth was, I *wanted* to kiss you... I couldn't help myself. And then when I did, it really shook me up. That's why I lashed out at you, my darling, and told you I wanted you to go. Because, damn it, you were the last woman I wanted to get tangled up with. My brother's widow...a woman who was convinced I'd all but ruined her husband's life. I was afraid that if you stayed on out here you'd eventually find out the truth and it would hurt you badly, and sully your memories of him. I didn't want that, Kate.'

She smiled mistily up at him. 'And now that I do know the truth, Nick,' she said softly, 'and you know that my memories and my marriage weren't as perfect as you thought, does that make a difference? Do you think you'll be able to forget what Jeremy did to you in the past and... and live with it? With *me*?' she amended with a gulp. 'Because, Nick, I do love you, with all my heart and body and soul. I didn't know what real love was until I met you... and I—I would hate to have what Jeremy did to you coming back to haunt us or—or ever coming between us.'

He pressed his lips to her cheek. 'Kate, my dearest, wonderful Kate, you can rest assured that will never happen. It's all in the past... forgotten. I haven't been scarred by it, I assure you. I'm tough. And remember, I had a lot of love as a child and as a young man. And Jeremy would have had it too, if he hadn't been so torn up inside. If he found any later with you, then I'm glad. And you should be glad too. And now, my darling,' he breathed against the silken skin of her throat, 'it's time we looked ahead. It's time for us now.'

'Oh, Nick, I don't deserve you,' she said in a choked voice. 'I've misjudged you and I've wronged you, all the way along the line. And yet you...'

'Hush! I'll say it again, Kate...it's our time now. You and me. And maybe one day there'll be three of us. Or four. Whatever comes, it'll be fine with me.'

'Oh, Nick, I——' The rest was crushed beneath his lips as his mouth came down on hers, not selfishly, clumsily, as she had come to expect from Jeremy, but persuasively, tormentingly, causing her to arch eagerly against him, a melting warmth flooding through her body, her hands sliding up yearningly into his thick black hair.

She was trembling, wanting him with a frantic need that this time, she knew, she wasn't going to deny. He was trembling too; she could feel the heat in him as he rolled her over on to her back, still kissing her. She felt a scorching flame pierce her deep inside as he lowered himself over her, the aroused thrust of his hips heightening the wild sensuality of his kiss as they allowed their long-pent-up feelings to flare out of control at last.

'I want to see you, Kate... all of you,' he gasped, tearing his lips away and dragging her to her feet. He was tugging at her clothes as he spoke, tossing them aside piece by piece, his own quickly following. As his eyes burned down the length of her silken body, he made a deep primitive sound in his throat, somewhere between a groan and a cry of hunger.

'You're even more beautiful than I dreamed, Kate.'

'You are too,' she whispered hoarsely, her body aching at the sight of his tautly muscled, beautifully proportioned body, his skin bronzed to a smooth polish that made her ache to touch him. There was a fever in her blood she had never known before, her whole body vibrating with the need to be close to him, to have him lose himself inside her.

'Come to me, Kate,' he said, and as he folded her in his arms she whimpered with a mixture of arousal and longing at the intimate contact of flesh against flesh, her hands stroking tremulously over his skin, registering with wonder his reaction to her touch, thrilling at her power to excite him and give him pleasure.

'I love you, Kate,' he groaned against her lips. He lowered her gently, almost reverently, on to the groundsheet and pressed his full length against her quivering body, drawing a moan from her as his lips seared a path down her throat, along the line of her collarbone to feather hot kisses over her body and between her breasts, moving with tantalising slowness to her throbbing nipple. As his mouth closed over the tender peak, his tongue circling and teasing, waves of erotic sensation stabbed to the very core of her being.

She felt his muscles flinch as she ran her hands down his back and writhed her hips in deliberate incitement, exulting in the vibrant power of his masculinity, the sensual heat of his skin, her body aching for more and more sensation. Nick seemed to have released a deep vein of sensuality in her that no one, not even her husband, had ever come near to touching.

Already, shamelessly, her body was melting in anticipation of even more intimate caresses, already longing to caress him with the same intimacy, overwhelmed by the flood of love and desire that poured through her, obliterating all restraints. Jeremy had always been in too much of a hurry to achieve his own gratification, too insensitive to any needs she might have to spend time arousing her the way Nick was doing now.

Now, with Nick, she found that she was the one who was impatient, realising in a blinding flash of revelation that something, some spark, some chemistry, must have been missing all along between Jeremy and herself, or she would have been excited by his mere touch, the mere brush of his lips, the way a mere look, a touch from Nick had been sufficient to inflame her.

'Love me, Nick, *please*,' she begged, her voice husky with longing. 'I want you so much!'

'I'm burning for you too,' he groaned against her lips. 'But I want this to last...I want to know all of you, Kate.'

There wasn't an inch of each other's body they didn't explore, and, by the time he moved to give her the release she craved, she was totally mindless, wave after wave of intense sensation breaking through her body, rising to a peak of almost anguished expectancy. She heard herself cry out, her body convulsing as the climax came, exploding like a star inside her, sending her spinning to heights she had never dreamed possible. As she floated off into a timeless, endless wonderland, she felt Nick shudder in a wild burst of passion and cry out her name in primeval possession. Then they both sighed and grew still, a tranquil peace spreading over them.

Eventually her eyes fluttered open, languidly meeting his. 'I never dreamed...it could be like that,' she murmured, her lips spreading into a smile of absolute satisfaction.

'Kate, my darling, this is only the beginning,' Nick assured her, his eyes still glazed with passion. As he reluctantly pulled her to her feet, he glanced up at the sky. Only the tip of the sun was visible above the towering cliffs. 'We'd better start heading back home, or it'll be dark before we get there.'

Home, Kate thought dreamily, as she started pulling on her clothes. *Our* home.

As she bent down afterwards to splash her face with cool water from the nearest rock pool a kookaburra laughed from somewhere high up in the trees.

She glanced up. 'I feel like laughing too,' she said. She was still smiling. She couldn't seem to stop. 'I'm just so happy.'

She felt Nick's hands slide over her shoulders, and she leant back against him, passion flaring anew at his touch, quivering all the way through her body. 'We deserve our happiness, Kate,' he said, brushing warm sensuous lips over the smooth nape of her neck.

She shivered in ecstasy. 'Let's get home...quickly,' she said huskily.

Let

HARLEQUIN ROMANCE®

take you

BACK TO THE RANCH

Come to SkyRim Ranch in Bison County, Nebraska!

Meet Abbie Hale, rancher's daughter—a woman who loves her family ranch and loves the ranching life. Then meet Yates Connley, the stranger who comes to SkyRim for Christmas....

Read Bethany Campbell's
The Man Who Came for Christmas,
our next Back to the Ranch title.
Available in December
wherever Harlequin books are sold.

RANCH7

**Fifty red-blooded, white-hot, true-blue hunks
from every State in the Union!**

Look for MEN MADE IN AMERICA! Written by some
of our most poplar authors, these stories feature fifty of
the strongest, sexiest men, each from a different state in
the union!

Two titles available every other month at your favorite
retail outlet.

In November, look for:

STRAIGHT FROM THE HEART by Barbara Delinsky
(Connecticut)
AUTHOR'S CHOICE by Elizabeth August (Delaware)

In January, look for:

DREAM COME TRUE by Ann Major (Florida)
WAY OF THE WILLOW by Linda Shaw (Georgia)

You won't be able to resist MEN MADE IN AMERICA!

Make Christmas a truly Romantic experience—with

◈ HARLEQUIN ROMANCE®

Wouldn't *you* love to kiss a tall, dark Texan under the mistletoe? Gwen does, in HOME FOR CHRISTMAS by Ellen James. Share the experience!

Wouldn't *you* love to kiss a sexy New Englander on a snowy Christmas morning? Angela does, in Shannon Waverly's CHRISTMAS ANGEL. Share the experience!

Look for both of these Christmas Romance titles, available in December wherever Harlequin Books are sold.

(And don't forget that Romance novels make great gifts! Easy to buy, easy to wrap and just the right size for a stocking stuffer. *And* they make a wonderful treat when you need a break from Christmas shopping, Christmas wrapping and stuffing stockings!)

1993 Keepsake

CHRISTMAS

Stories

Capture the spirit and romance of Christmas with KEEPSAKE CHRISTMAS STORIES, a collection of three stories by favorite historical authors. The perfect Christmas gift!

Don't miss these heartwarming stories, available in November wherever Harlequin books are sold:

ONCE UPON A CHRISTMAS by Curtiss Ann Matlock
A FAIRYTALE SEASON by Marianne Willman
TIDINGS OF JOY by Victoria Pade

ADD A TOUCH OF ROMANCE TO YOUR HOLIDAY SEASON WITH KEEPSAKE CHRISTMAS STORIES!

HX93

When the only time you have for yourself is...

STOLEN *moments* ™

Christmas is such a busy time—with shopping, decorating, writing
cards, trimming trees, wrapping gifts....

When you do have a few *stolen moments* to call your own, treat yourself
to a brand-new *short* novel. Relax with one of our Stocking Stuffers—
or with all six!

Each STOLEN MOMENTS title
is a complete and original contemporary romance that's the perfect
length for the busy woman of the nineties! Especially at Christmas...

And they make perfect **stocking stuffers**, too! (For your mother,
grandmother, daughters, friends, co-workers, neighbors, aunts,
cousins—all the other women in your life!)

Look for the STOLEN MOMENTS display in December

STOCKING STUFFERS:

HIS MISTRESS Carrie Alexander
DANIEL'S DECEPTION Marie DeWitt
SNOW ANGEL Isolde Evans
THE FAMILY MAN Danielle Kelly
THE LONE WOLF Ellen Rogers
MONTANA CHRISTMAS Lynn Russell

HSM2